THE BILLIONAIRE'S SECRETS

A Novel

MEADOW TAYLOR

HarperCollins*Publishers*Ltd

The Billionaire's Secrets
Copyright © 2012 by Gina Buonaguro and Janice Kirk
All rights reserved.

Published by HarperCollins Publishers Ltd

First published in Canada by HarperCollins Publishers Ltd
in an e-book original edition: 2012
This mass market paperback editon: 2017

HarperCollins books may be purchased for educational, business,
or sales promotional use through our Special Markets Department.

HarperCollins Publishers Ltd
2 Bloor Street East, 20th Floor
Toronto, Ontario, Canada
M4W 1A8

www.harpercollins.ca

Library and Archives Canada Cataloguing in Publication
information is available upon request.

ISBN 978-1-44342-273-4

Printed and bound in the United States
QUAD 10 9 8 7 6 5 4 3 2 1

For Ellen in Atlanta

"All my heart is yours, sir: it belongs to you; and with you it would remain, were fate to exile the rest of me from your presence forever."
CHARLOTTE BRONTË, JANE EYRE

THE BILLIONAIRE'S SECRETS

CHAPTER 1

THE FOG WAS SO THICK THAT CHLOE DIDN'T see the car until it was almost on top of her. Certainly, she didn't have time to react. One moment she was slogging along the road bent under the weight of her bags and suitcases, and the next moment she was eye to eye with a Rolls-Royce hood ornament.

The car ground to a halt inches from her, and she could feel the warmth of the engine against her face. Blinded by the headlights, frozen with shock, she stood rooted to the spot, not even sure for a moment whether she had been hit or not. Then she heard the car door open and a man's voice boomed out of the darkness. "What are you doing? Are you trying to get yourself killed?"

His voice penetrated the shock. Finally able to react, she let out a cry. She dropped her bags and staggered back from the car, only to trip over one of her suitcases and fall on her behind. "I . . . I didn't see you," she gasped. She raised her arm to shield her eyes from the glare of the lights, but still she could not see the owner of the voice.

Suddenly she became aware that while he wasn't

visible, *she* was definitely in the spotlight. Her coat and skirt were bunched up around her hips, her legs spread at an immodest angle. She felt a hole open up in her stocking over her knee. One of her cases had sprung open, and bright white bras, slips, and panties spilled onto the road. Feeling her face flush with embarrassment, she grabbed at the escaped lingerie and stuffed it into her old suitcase as she scrambled to her feet.

Without the headlights shining in her eyes, she was no longer blinded, though what she saw almost made her fall over again.

He was standing by the side of his car, his hands in the pockets of his long black cashmere coat, opened to reveal a pair of expensive jeans and a designer sweater. He was not wearing a hat, and his hair was black and thick. *Hair to run your fingers through*, she thought absurdly. The dense fog and the dark night suited him. Sexy, dark, mysterious, exuding wealth, he was so handsome that she wondered for a moment whether the car really had hit her. Maybe she was dead. But was he some heavenly angel or the devil himself? He looked angry enough to be the devil. His eyes flashed fire and his movie-star features were set in hard lines. "What the hell are you doing here, anyway?" he asked, his voice low and cold. "This is private property. And you are trespassing."

Nervously, Chloe took a step back. "I'm looking for Widow's Cliff," she stammered. "It's the name of a house—"

"I know it's the name of a house," he interrupted impatiently. "It happens to be *my* house. And who are you?"

"You're Gaelan Byrne?" she asked in dismay. Perhaps she would have preferred him to be the devil. Preferable to meet the devil on a dark country road than to find out this man—so good-looking and yet so angry, downright rude, even—was her new employer!

"And who wants to know? You're not another damned paparazzo, are you? I'm sick and tired of you people—why do you think I live way the hell out here?" The night was cold, and his words came out in clouds, merging with the fog.

"Paparazzo? No, no, of course not. I'm Chloe Winters." As he still didn't seem to understand, she added uncertainly, "The new tutor?" She started to extend her hand but decided against it, instead putting them both in her pockets. He didn't look like he wanted to shake her hand. The interviewer had told her he was a widower, so she had expected someone older. Not even the fact that he had a six-year-old child had deterred her image of him as grey-haired. Old enough to be her father, old enough that a romantic relationship would be completely out of the question. After her last boyfriend, she wasn't sure she ever wanted to be involved with another man again.

He said nothing, his expression morphing from anger into distaste. Maybe she didn't need to worry—his bad manners were very quickly making up for his good looks. But then, bad manners were not very appealing in an employer, either. She felt a premonition of impending disaster.

"For your little girl," she explained further with a sigh. Did he even know he'd advertised for a tutor? "I thought someone was supposed to meet me at the St. John's airport. Nobody came. I figured maybe the car had broken down or something, and I didn't have your phone number . . . I had to take a bus . . ." She was on a roll now, reciting the litany of disasters that had occurred since she left Boston that morning.

Really—she was the one who should be angry. She was the one who had stood around the airport all afternoon before catching a shuttle to Puffin's Cove. Then the local bus driver had dropped her on the side of the highway, telling her the house was still a mile down a dirt road. Then this man almost ran her over with his fancy car. Her stockings were torn, she was freezing . . .

Suddenly, he started to laugh, but there was no warmth in it, and his eyes still shot lightning bolts at her. He was definitely laughing *at* her, not with her.

"It's not funny," she protested, feeling a slightly hysterical edge creep into her voice.

He stopped laughing. "You're right, it's not funny," he said soberly. "It's infuriating." He threw up his hands. "I can't believe my assistant hired you. Not only do you walk down the centre of dark roads not paying any attention, you can't even arrive on the right day."

"It's the right day," she said defensively. "It's April the seventh today."

"And you were to start on the seventeenth."

"No, the seventh," she insisted. "The man in Boston who interviewed me told me the seventh."

"That man in Boston is my second-in-command. I can assure you he has never made a mistake in his life." He leaned against the car and crossed his arms. He looked her up and down as if he had never seen anything that disgusted him more. Chloe wouldn't have been surprised if he found the squashed bugs on his windshield more appealing. "Let me correct that. Never made a mistake until he hired you. What did you do? Flash those sexy legs at him?"

Well, at least she had scored points for having nice legs. Or had she? Wasn't he accusing her of seducing his assistant? She opened her mouth to make some sort of retort in her defence, but no words came to her.

He looked pleased that he had rendered her speechless. He opened the car door, then turned to her. Chloe was very aware of his dark, smouldering eyes locked on hers. "You've got half a mile more," he said coolly. "I have a meeting tonight, and you've made me late. The housekeeper will let you in. Now, pay attention to where you're going. If you miss the house, you'll walk right off the cliff. And you wouldn't want to do that—it's a three-hundred-foot drop onto the rocks, and it's been done before."

It was obvious that he was waiting for her to get out of his way. Mortified, Chloe grabbed her bags and struggled to the edge of the road. And while he had sounded as if he would be delighted if she fell off a cliff, the least he could have done was offer to take her bags!

"Consider it a chance to redeem yourself," he said, watching her impassively. "If you get to the house alive, I'll reconsider my decision to fire you on the spot." He got into the car and put it into gear. She stood among her bags and watched helplessly as the huge silver car rolled past her. He didn't even look at her, and within moments the tail lights were swallowed by the fog.

The sound of the car soon faded too, and in the quiet she could hear the distant roar of the ocean. Angry tears pricked at her eyes as she arranged her bags in her arms and continued on the road to the house. It was so dark and misty she couldn't see more than a foot in front of her. Conscious now of the threat of cars, she walked on the edge where the gravel met the grass. She wasn't too worried about dropping off a cliff—the bus driver had said to keep to the road and it would lead her right to the door. As she walked, she thought back to Gaelan's words. *You'll walk right off the cliff, and you wouldn't want to do that.* It was pretty obvious that if she did, it wouldn't bother him in the least.

How had she gotten herself into this mess? She hadn't even started her new job, and already everything was going wrong. That is, if she still had a job. It wasn't looking too hopeful at the moment. It surely wasn't what she'd pictured when she had answered the ad in the back of the magazine for retired teachers. Not that she was retired. She had, in fact, been fired. All thanks to Shawn.

But the ad had looked like the answer to her problems—a job and a way of putting distance between herself and Shawn. She had met Shawn on a whitewater rafting adventure trip in Maine a year earlier. He was a teacher too, and their relationship seemed natural. Before long, they were living together. A few months later, she lost her job at a private school due to declining enrolment. The financial crisis had hit the Boston banking community hard, with many families pulling their kids from the school. Out of a job and short of money, she was also forced to leave her master's in education program a few credits shy of her degree. Luckily, she found another teaching position at a nearby boarding academy. True, she lied on her resumé about already having that degree, but it was a requirement for the job, and what else was she to do? Her parents couldn't help—the stock market crash had wiped out almost all their retirement savings, and now they were forced to work at the Home Depot on Cape Cod to make ends meet. The headmaster never would have even known—if it hadn't been for Shawn.

Shawn had asked her to marry him, and she was close to saying yes when he told her he couldn't see them having a family. In her heart, she realized this was a deal breaker—she adored children. That's why she had become a teacher, and she couldn't imagine her future without a few of her own. And at thirty-two, she didn't want to wait much longer to start. But when she told him this, he'd become petulant, swearing that if it was so important to her, why hadn't she told him before? She had, but clearly he didn't think it important enough to remember. The fights had been terrible, and he'd grudgingly agreed in the end that maybe one child would be okay. But Chloe knew this wasn't good enough. She didn't want to raise a child with a father who was only "okay" with the idea, so she broke off the relationship. Shawn was furious. Still unable to grasp the simple concept of how important a family was to her, he became convinced it had to be more. Certain now she was having an affair, he informed her new headmaster about her lack of a degree. The headmaster wasted no time in firing her. And as if that weren't revenge enough, all their friends sided with him, so not only was she boyfriendless and childless, she was also jobless and friendless.

She didn't have the nerve to ask for a reference—even though her work record and ratings were otherwise impeccable—and things were looking pretty bleak until she saw the ad in the magazine. *Looking for a mature retired female teacher as a companion/tutor for a six-year-old girl in a secluded oceanside setting in Newfoundland,* the ad had read. *Must live in and start immediately.* She'd pictured herself taking long walks along the ocean, early nights, easy work. She was used to teaching twenty children at a time—just one would be a breeze!

She had answered the ad (quite honestly adding that she was not retired) and to her surprise received an answer right away. She had gone for the interview the very next day at the Boston offices of Byrne Enterprises. From the signs in the lobby, she determined that there were also offices in Montreal and San Francisco. The man who interviewed her introduced himself as Marcus and his employer was often away on business. He asked her several questions about her own education and interests and seemed especially pleased that, thanks to her French-Canadian mother, she spoke fluent French. Much to her relief, he did not mention references. He hired her on the spot and asked her to start on April 7. Or so she had thought.

At least the bus driver had been right. The road did lead right to the house. She saw the glow of lights through the fog only steps before reaching the door. The sound of the ocean battering against the rocks filled the air. The cliff was very close now. She put down her bags and paused to regain her breath before ringing the bell. The door was huge, made up of heavy oak panels. There was no window, and Chloe thought it looked like the door to a castle, not a house. She looked up at the facade to where it disappeared into the fog and decided that perhaps it *was* a castle. It was built with huge stone blocks, and light flowed from diamond-paned leaded windows. In her imagination she had pictured a cozy wooden house, its siding weathered with salt and wind, like the ones in calendar pictures of the New England coast. But this was anything but cozy. Though beautiful, it was downright daunting, and when she rang the bell she wondered for a moment if it would be answered by a hunchback named Igor.

But it wasn't Igor. It was a little girl with blond curls

and an angelic face. *My new student*, Chloe thought, her heart already opening up to the child. But the girl obviously didn't feel the same way. She took one look at Chloe, her eyes widened with fear, and she started to scream.

GAELAN NAVIGATED HIS way through the fog, cursing it, his friend and assistant Marcus, the occasion that had made this trip necessary, and the woman he had just left on the side of the road. He shouldn't have been so hard on her. After all, she'd just about been run over. He'd probably scared her half to death—and to then tell her about the cliff as if he didn't care whether she walked right off it had been pretty cold, no matter what her motives for being here.

It was just that, all things combined, he had been pretty furious. The sight of her in his headlights had been a shock, and even though he had immediately slammed on his brakes, he had been sure he was going to hit her. Really, he had only yelled at her because his adrenalin had gone into overdrive.

Well, at first. What was it about her that had immediately started to irritate him? It was the way she looked up at him from the ground, he decided. The way she scrambled around picking up her things, pulling down her coat, embarrassed and modest. After Colleen, these glimpses of vulnerability in a woman no longer brought out the gentlemanly side of him but rather made him instantly angry.

Fair enough. Colleen's vulnerability had turned out to be a calculated game that was intended to trap him. Marcus constantly reminded him that not all women were like her, but Gaelan knew that when one was as rich as he was, the Colleens of the world beat a pathway to the door. The moment they got a whiff of his money they were on him like bloodhounds—even ones who had a considerable amount of their own. Where money was concerned, apparently there was never too much. And who was to say this girl wasn't one of them? Why would she have applied for the job otherwise? No attractive young woman would want to isolate herself like this—unless she had something in mind. He was sure he had fortune-hunter-proofed his ad. He had been more than clear that he wanted a *mature* retired teacher. Short of putting *no one under the age of sixty-five need apply*, how much clearer could he have been? And he *had* been that clear with Marcus.

He hit the steering wheel with one of his gloved hands and cursed Marcus yet again. He and Marcus had discussed this ad nauseam: Someone old enough not to get any ideas about wooing her way into his bed and fortune. Someone old enough that he, in a weak moment, would not find himself looking at her with lust. He had in mind a sexless seventy-year-old in support hose and tweed, as much a grandmother for Sophia as a tutor.

There would be no more repeats of Colleen or that last one, who had had a genuine enough teaching degree yet was not only doing her best to seduce him but also selling stories to a gossip magazine. *What really happened to the sexy billionaire's wife*? the headline had read. As if he kept Colleen locked up in the attic or something. And here Marcus sent this girl—and one with legs that could drive a man crazy! What part of *at least seventy*, *support hose*, and *retired* didn't he get?

And it wasn't just about him, either. It was about Sophia. Every time one of these women came along, the first thing they did was worm their way into Sophia's affections. The girl was so desperate for a mother, she fell head over heels in love with every woman who showed her the least bit of attention, and then he had to play the bad guy and kick them out. Best he act immediately. She'd leave first thing in the morning. Sophia should be in bed by now—with any luck she wouldn't even meet this one.

The fog was lighter on the highway, and it wasn't long before he reached the town of Puffin's Cove. He didn't want to be here, but he had promised to put in a show-ing at the town council meeting to support a motion on declaring a nearby wetland an environmentally protected region. Gaelan sometimes found himself at odds with some of the local businesses and politicians who believed that everything, including the environment, was fair game when it came to making money. He saw it instead as everyone's duty to make sure there was still a planet around for future generations, and he was seen by some as an environmental champion.

However, he found it hard to concentrate on the meeting, which turned out to be even more contentious than he had predicted. All he could think of was this woman, worming her way into Sophia's good graces as she planned how she would worm her way into his. Yes, better to get rid of her sooner rather than later. The child didn't need to feel like she was being deserted yet again. Damn, he was going to kill Marcus!

CHLOE STEPPED BACK from the door and tried to think of a suitable reaction to the screaming girl. Fortunately, an older woman appeared in the foyer. She too seemed taken aback for a moment at the sight of Chloe, but at least she didn't start to scream. She looped a strong arm around the girl. "Stop that, child. You'll rub me nerves right raw!" The girl stopped instantly, but she stayed within the protective circle of the woman's arms, regarding Chloe now with a mixture of interest and distrust.

"Can I help you?" the woman asked Chloe. Chloe couldn't even begin to guess her age. She was a large woman and wore what Chloe's mother always called a "housedress," a shapeless garment of printed cotton for doing housework. She had thick white hair that was pulled back into a bun at the nape of her neck, and her florid face was criss-crossed with deep wrinkles. Her smile was bright, and her eyes twinkled with good humour.

Chloe gave them both her bravest smile. "Hi. My name is Chloe," she said in her brightest schoolteacher voice. "I don't know whether I've arrived on the right day or not, but I'm Sophia's new teacher."

"Goodness gracious, girl!" the woman exclaimed, opening the door wider, letting out a seductive flood of warmth. Behind her, Chloe glimpsed a huge wood-panelled hall, adding to the impression that Widow's Cliff was indeed a castle. "You're early. We weren't expecting you for another week and a half!"

"I think I got my dates mixed up," Chloe said weakly.

"Well, never you mind, you come right in."

"Thank you," Chloe said gratefully. She picked up her bags and set them down inside the door. "You must be Sophia," she said to the little girl.

Sophia nodded her head vigorously, all signs of distrust melting like an icicle in the sun.

"I'm sorry I frightened you," Chloe said.

Sophia smiled. "I was just playing," she said.

Chloe glanced at the housekeeper.

"Like I say, she rubs me nerves," she said without any sign of irritation. She spoke with a distinctive Newfoundland accent, musical and lilting, reminiscent of her Irish ancestors. "She probably saw you there with your hair like a birch broom in fits and thought you was a ghost or something. I must say you gave me a start myself. And I wasn't expecting anyone as young as you!"

Chloe laughed as much at the housekeeper's expressions as at the idea of Sophia thinking she was a ghost.

"Did you really think I was a ghost?" she asked the girl.

Sophia shook her head, and Chloe smiled at her. She liked her already and wondered how much of the immediate need she felt to protect Sophia had to do with the girl's father.

The housekeeper started to pick up the bags, but Chloe stopped her. "Please, don't pick them up. I'll move them. Maybe Sophia can show me my room." Silently she prayed that it would still be her room tomorrow and that Gaelan Byrne would not send her back on the first plane out of St. John's.

"Okay, okay," said the woman. "But first, we'll have a cup'a tea. You look tired and froze right through."

"A cup of tea sounds lovely," Chloe said. The house-keeper took her coat and hung it on a coat rack before leading the way to the kitchen.

"I should introduce myself," she said. "My name is Windy."

"I'm pleased to meet you, Windy. I like your name. It's very pretty."

"It suits me. I was born in a gale, my husband died when his fishing boat went down in a gale, and I'm sure I'll be blown to heaven on a gale." She laughed at her own joke, and Chloe joined in.

The kitchen was beautiful and warm. At one end of the room a fire blazed in a large fireplace, while the other end held state-of-the-art appliances that would be the delight of any cook. In between was a long harvest table surrounded by cane-seated chairs. Spread across the table were several children's books, a newspaper, and some children's drawings.

"Did you draw this?" Chloe asked, picking up one of the sheets of paper and holding it out to Sophia. A picture of a house on a cliff, it was dark and brooding, with storm clouds gathering above it and a wild sea smashing below.

Sophia nodded a bit hesitantly, as if wondering whether she was about to get in trouble.

"It's very good," Chloe said sincerely. Actually, the drawings were excellent for a child of six. Sophia was obviously very talented. "Is it Widow's Cliff?"

Sophia nodded, more enthusiastically this time. She picked up a picture of a cat and handed it to Chloe. "I drew this one too. It's my cat, Cookies. He's upstairs in my room right now. You can come up and meet him."

Chloe took it from the child. "I'd love to. Do you draw a lot?"

Sophia shrugged. "Sometimes."

Windy placed steaming mugs of tea and a plate of homemade chocolate chip cookies on the table. Chloe was pleased when Sophia chose to sit next to her. She felt warm and happy. *Oh please, don't send me away*! she prayed silently, not knowing if it was a higher power or Gaelan Byrne she was praying to.

"Can I have two cookies, Windy?" Sophia asked.

"Yes, dear," Windy said.

"Can Chloe?" she said.

Windy laughed. "Chloe is the guest, and she can have as many as she wants."

Chloe complimented Windy on the cookies and tea and listened attentively to Sophia as she talked about her drawings. Except for the house picture, they were all of moose, bears, and other animals, and Chloe concluded that Sophia's true passion was animals, not drawing. Nonetheless, the girl was talented, and Chloe vowed to encourage her. That is, if she were allowed to stay.

"Do we start school tomorrow?" Sophia asked hopefully.

Chloe suppressed a sigh with a sip of tea. "I don't know, Sophia. I still have to talk to your father. I'm not sure I'll be your new teacher. I'd like to be, but it's up to him."

Windy looked like she was about to object, but Chloe shot her what she hoped was a warning glance.

"You are my new teacher! He promised!" Sophia objected. She crossed her arms and stuck out her bottom lip in the universal sign of sulkiness.

Chloe put her arm around the girl's shoulders and gave her a quick hug. "Well, you keep your fingers crossed then that everything works out." Chloe always found it difficult to explain the foibles of adults to children. It was a hard lesson for them to learn that adults could not always be relied on to keep their promises. "How about you show me my room? I could use some help with my suitcases."

Sophia immediately brightened. "Okay," she said pulling away from Chloe and running out into the hall. Chloe had been about to follow, but Windy put a hand on her arm to stop her.

"Do you not want to stay here?" she asked in a low voice.

"Of course I do," Chloe said earnestly, casting a glance at Sophia. "I already love it here. I just don't know about Mr. Byrne. I met him on the road on the way in, and he didn't seem very happy to see me."

"Oh, that's just Gaelan. You can't put too much stock in that. He's an odd duck for sure. Doesn't know what's good for him anymore. He's been hurt real badly. Ever since his wife—" Windy stopped short as Sophia picked up the heaviest of Chloe's bags.

"Sophia, put that down! It's much too heavy for you."

Chloe thought that Windy must be referring to the death of Gaelan Byrne's wife. Of course—he must still be in mourning, and wasn't anger one of the stages of grief?

"I can carry it," Sophia insisted.

"Windy's right," Chloe said, taking the bag from the girl. "You carry this one." She pointed to the bag whose contents had so recently been dumped on the road. "It isn't so heavy."

Windy picked up the remaining bag that held the books and school supplies Chloe had brought. "How did you carry this all yourself?"

"It wasn't too bad," Chloe lied. She didn't want to explain how she had expected to be picked up at the airport and how Gaelan had left her standing on the drive with all of her bags.

An open staircase wound up one side of the hallway to a second-floor landing that looked over it. Long halls branched off on either side of the landing, confirming Chloe's suspicion that the house was more like a castle. "Do you clean this house all by yourself?"

"No, thank heavens," Windy said as she led the way down one of these halls. "Two local girls come in every morning. Really, I just look after the cooking and washing up. And Sophia, of course." They reached the end of the hall, and Windy opened the last door on the right.

The room was huge, and out of one corner jutted a circular area surrounded by windows. "A turret!" Chloe exclaimed. She couldn't believe this was her room—it was like something out of a historical romance novel! Her and Shawn's old apartment in Boston was a broom closet next to this. Windy went over and lit the fireplace. Facing the fireplace was a chintz-covered loveseat, and Chloe imagined herself curled up with a good book. The floors were dark planks covered with excellent Middle Eastern carpets. But the icing on the cake was an antique canopy bed complete with bed curtains. Not in her wildest dreams had Chloe imagined herself in surroundings like this. She went to the turret windows and pulled back the drapes, but there was only blackness.

"The view is beautiful," Windy said, setting the fireplace screen before the fire. "Hopefully, the fog will clear tonight, and you'll get a chance to enjoy it by and by in the morning." Chloe hoped so too, but she was sure Gaelan Byrne was a bigger barrier to enjoying the view.

The fog would eventually clear, but whether she would be here when that happened was the bigger question.

"Can I put your clothes away?" Sophia asked.

"Not tonight, sweetie," Chloe said. "I'm really too tired." She didn't want to bring up the possibility she wouldn't be around long enough to make it worthwhile.

"I think we should leave Chloe in peace for a while," Windy added. She turned to Chloe. "Your bathroom is directly across the hall. Why don't you have a nice hot bath?"

"I don't want to miss Mr. Byrne when he comes back," Chloe said. She really didn't want to be in the bathtub when he booted her out. It would be so undignified, to say the least!

Windy looked at her watch. "He won't be home for at least another hour. You have time."

"Okay then, I will." A bath would feel good. She would put on something nice and do her makeup. Perhaps she could convince Gaelan to give her a chance to prove herself.

"And you," Windy said to Sophia, who had climbed up on the bed and was rearranging all the many pillows and cushions. "You should have your own bath and get ready for bed. It's way past your bedtime. And you're just getting over a cold. You know the doctor told you to go to bed on time and get lots of sleep."

"I want to see Daddy too," Sophia insisted.

Windy sighed indulgently. "Okay, but you're still going to have your bath. A nice warm one, right full of Epsom salts for that cold."

"All right," Sophia agreed, as if she were doing Windy a favour, and jumped down off the bed.

After they had left, Chloe opened her suitcases. She blushed at the thought of Gaelan Byrne seeing her underthings spread out on the road. Some of them now had smudges from the dirt. She sighed, stuffing the soiled bras and panties into a pocket in the lining of the suitcase, and searched for something clean. She would have all the time in the world to do laundry when she got sent back to Boston. Then, suddenly, the full implications of losing this job hit home. She had moved out of her and Shawn's apartment in Boston weeks ago and couldn't bear the thought of staying again on her cousin Anthony's couch, she had no money beyond her small savings, her parents had their own financial problems, and she had no other job prospects. She had to keep this job. Dream job or not, this was a matter of survival.

She picked out a simple black wool dress that she knew was flattering and a pair of black stockings. From the underthings that had survived the mishap, she chose a pair of lacy white panties and a bra. If she had to appeal to the sensual side of Gaelan Byrne to keep this job, she would do it, no matter how loudly the feminist in her objected.

She headed across the hall to her bathroom. It was every bit as luxurious as her room, with antique fixtures and polished brass taps, but as she soaked in the deep, old-fashioned claw-foot tub, she found it hard to relax and enjoy her surroundings—she was too focused on her upcoming meeting with Gaelan.

Perhaps she had just caught him at a bad moment. Windy had said he was an "odd duck," but her tone seemed to indicate that everything would be fine. It was important not to panic. Meeting him again would be like going on another job interview. She would be polite and calm. She would shake his hand and introduce herself formally. Perhaps it would be better not to make any reference to their meeting on the road. Just start at the beginning. Surely, once he spoke to her, he would realize she was perfect for the job. Plus, she had the vote of Sophia. Surely, once he saw how much his child liked her . . .

She washed her hair and got out of the tub, wrapping herself in a thick white towel. She blow-dried her hair, letting it fall in natural waves around her shoulders. Her hair, she felt, was her best feature, thick and shiny and strawberry blond. Back in the bedroom, she dressed and put on some lipstick. She was as prepared as she ever would be.

Gaelan Byrne opened the door just as Chloe reached the landing overlooking the entrance hall. Wanting a moment to gather her courage before meeting him, she stepped back into the shadows of the hall. Just then, Sophia, dressed in her nightgown, ran out of the kitchen toward her father. "Daddy!" she called, running toward him. "Chloe's here!"

"I know, Sophia," he said, pulling off his gloves and throwing them onto a chair. He took off his coat and tossed it on the chair as well. "And how many times do

I have to tell you to stop calling me Daddy? Gaelan will do just fine. You're not a baby anymore."

"Sorry," Sophia said sheepishly.

Chloe was shocked. Where were the hugs and kisses fathers were supposed to greet their children with when they came home? And what was this about not calling him Daddy? Chloe still called her father Dad and always would. She couldn't imagine even Shawn being this cold. How could Gaelan Byrne have so little affection for his own child?

"Why aren't you in bed?" he asked sharply. "You were supposed to be in bed two hours ago."

"Windy said I could stay up 'cause Chloe's here."

"Okay, so now that you've told me she's here, it's time you went to bed. Where's Windy?"

"She's in the kitchen, and I want Chloe to put me to bed!"

"Sophia," he said impatiently, "be reasonable, please. It has been a long day. And you know what the doctor said."

"I don't want you to send Chloe away," she said stubbornly. "I want her to be my teacher."

"Who said I was going to send Chloe away?" he demanded.

"Chloe did."

"She did, did she? And where is Chloe now?"

Chloe decided this was her cue. She stepped out of the shadows of the hall onto the landing toward the stairs. "I'm here," she said.

She felt Gaelan's eyes on her as she walked down the stairs. Sophia ran over to her and held her arms up. Chloe gave her a quick hug. "Go find Windy and tell her it's time for bed. I need to talk with your daddy." She emphasized the word *daddy*, hoping Gaelan would notice.

"I don't want you to go!" Sophia sounded desperate and close to tears.

"That's what I have to talk to your daddy about. So go to bed and try not to worry, okay? I'll come in and say good night in a little while."

"But what if I'm asleep?"

"I'll say good night anyway, and you'll hear me in your dreams." Certainly, Gaelan would allow that much.

"Good night, Sophia," Gaelan said firmly, and to Chloe's surprise, he gave her a quick hug and kissed her on the cheek. She hugged him back before going off meekly to find Windy.

While the hug seemed to satisfy Sophia, it only strengthened Chloe's resolve to stay. She couldn't help but think it was only for show. What a poor little rich girl Sophia was! Isolated in this great big house with no school friends, no mother, and a father who was so cold he didn't even allow her to call him Daddy. If the child was prone to temper tantrums, it was no surprise—she was starved for affection.

"I overheard you speaking with Sophia," Chloe said in the neutral professional voice she used in parent-teacher interviews. "I thought it best not to get her hopes up that I was staying."

"I see. Well, it didn't take you long to turn her into a good advocate on your behalf," he said cynically.

"I can assure you that was not the intention. I was simply trying to spare her feelings."

"Yes, I'm sure." He sounded unconvinced. "Come into my study. I'd like to have a drink."

He led the way to a room on the main floor and, as she entered, Chloe realized it was directly below her bedroom, the alcove surrounded with windows part of the same turret. The rest of the room looked like the sort of study seen in movies set in manor houses in the English countryside, all dark panelling and leather furniture. He closed the door behind her and lit a fire under the logs in the fireplace before pouring a drink from a bottle on the mantel. He did not ask her to sit, and she stood awkwardly in the doorway.

"Would you like a Scotch?" he asked, and it occurred to Chloe it was perhaps the first polite gesture he had made toward her.

"Yes, please," she said.

"I don't have any ice."

Is that an apology? she wondered. *Perhaps there's a man with a heart under there after all,* she thought sarcastically.

"That's fine. I like mine neat."

"Not very schoolmarm-like of you," he said, pouring her a glass. "Although I approve. Good Scotch should never be watered down." He held the glass out toward her, and she left her post by the door to take the

25

drink from his hand. He did not relinquish the drink immediately, holding it for a moment as he looked at her critically. She was very aware of his closeness. Her head did not quite reach his shoulder, and she was looking at the button of his ivory-coloured shirt. He smelled of the outdoors, of the ocean air. She could sense the power of his body and was again reminded of the ocean, so powerful, moody, and restless. It was attractive and seductive—she couldn't deny that—but it was also dangerous, full of pitfalls, susceptible to sudden storms. Definitely someone not to get involved with. *Not if you didn't want your heart broken . . .*

He relinquished his hold on the glass, and she stepped back as if to remove herself from the field of magnetism, daring to meet his eyes. He was looking back at her with a somewhat triumphant gleam in his eye, as if he had just proved something. She wondered what. She turned away and studied the photographs on the wall over the mantel. They were nature photographs, with whales, birds, and icebergs as the main subjects. They were excellent, and she was surprised to see they were signed *G. Byrne*. These photographs showed a sensitive side to Gaelan Byrne that he didn't seem to care to show any other way.

GAELAN MOVED TO his desk and picked up the receiver of his phone to check his messages. He only half listened to them, most of his mind concentrating on Chloe, who was still watching the fire. Or at least pretending to. He knew she was thinking about something else entirely. He had felt it only moments before, as he handed her the Scotch—felt it himself, too. The unmistakable tug of attraction.

She certainly is beautiful, he thought. Not in the glamorous model way like Colleen, but in a more classic way, like a Victorian painting, all soft, enticing curves. Made him wonder if he shouldn't just go for it—a teacher for Sophia, a mistress for himself.

It wasn't natural, this self-imposed celibacy. He missed the feel of a woman's body beneath his hands and the touch of her lips on his skin . . . *Damn*, he thought as his body started to react to these erotic thoughts. *If only it were that easy*. He remembered his attraction to Colleen. It had seemed so easy then, too—no premonition of the horrors to come.

The last message was from Marcus. "Just checking my book, Gaelan. I made a mistake. Sophia's new teacher arrived in Newfoundland today. I don't know how I got the dates mixed up. I hope she's not still standing at the airport." There was a pause, and Gaelan heard the smile in his friend's voice as he continued. "I know she's not quite what you're expecting, but she'll be perfect for you both. Talk to you soon."

Christ, Gaelan thought. He was going to kill Marcus! But first he had to get rid of this gold digger. And he

CHAPTER 2

GAELAN SLAMMED THE RECEIVER INTO ITS cradle and looked up to see Chloe eyeing him nervously. *Good*, he thought, not without guilt. *She's scared of me. This'll be easy.* In a few minutes he would be able to forget about this woman, sexy curves and all, and he could go about finding someone for Sophia who wasn't going to exploit the child's affections to get to his money.

"Ms. Winters," he began in a calculatingly cold and formal voice. "I'm a busy man, and I'd like to keep this brief. I cannot possibly employ you, and I think it would be best for everyone if you left first thing in the morning."

He expected her to nod, give up, and leave. Instead, she drew herself up to her full five and a half feet and addressed him in a haughty voice. "I think it's only fair that you explain to me why you can't employ me. I came a long way to take this job."

Her tone infuriated him. "I don't have to explain myself to you," he said aloofly. "I've met you, and I don't want you here. End of story."

29

But Chloe didn't give up. "Why did you let Marcus do the hiring if you didn't trust his judgment?"

"Did you not hear me? I think I've made it perfectly clear that I do not have to explain myself." He wasn't used to having his decisions questioned, and he couldn't believe she was criticizing how he ran his affairs. Well, anything that steeled his resolve to get rid of the woman was welcome. "This meeting is over, Ms. Winters. You will be taken to the airport first thing tomorrow."

Gaelan threw back the contents of his glass of Scotch and looked longingly at the bottle on the mantel. It had been the sort of day that made you want to end it in a drunken oblivion. Certainly one more wouldn't hurt. He went to the mantel and refilled his glass before returning to his position behind the desk. She was watching him, and he suddenly found himself thinking how kissable her lips looked. He changed his mind about getting drunk. One more Scotch and he wasn't going to be able to concentrate.

"Isn't it a breach of contract to dismiss me like this?" Chloe's voice penetrated his thoughts. "I was, after all, hired for a year."

"Are you threatening me with a lawsuit?" he said, her kissable lips quickly forgotten.

"I didn't say that," Chloe objected sharply. "I was asking you a question. I have rights, you know." It was such a naive statement that Gaelan found himself wanting to laugh.

"Well, I wouldn't suggest that you try and exercise

them, as I have sufficient funds to mop the floor with you should you try." She had that look that said, *Oh yes? That's what* you *think*, and Gaelan found himself amused. She was determined, he had to give her that— which of course was why she was too dangerous to keep around. Nonetheless, he felt a grudging admiration. Most women had tried to get into his bed either by acting innocent and helpless or by playing the sex kitten. He didn't know which irritated him the most. This was at least a variation on the theme.

Gaelan suppressed a smile. "Fortunately for you, I've already decided to compensate you for your trouble." Of course he hadn't, but she didn't need to know that. It would, however, make an interesting test. If he was right about her, he was sure the offer would—one, get rid of her, and two, confirm that it was his money she had been interested in all along. "How's six months' pay for not lifting a finger?"

He watched with grim satisfaction as her eyes grew larger. "I thought that would do the trick," he said quietly but not without a certain disappointment. *Hope, as they say, springs eternal*, he thought.

Then her face changed. For a second he thought she was going to fly across the desk at him. "Do you think I'm here just for the money?" she asked indignantly. "I came because I love children and I love to teach."

"Then why aren't you teaching in a school?" he said, deciding that his test probably hadn't proved a thing. He could see her hesitate, and he knew she wasn't being straight with him. She was hiding something from him—he could see it in those beautiful green eyes of hers. "Why are you here?" he demanded.

"I wanted a change," she said, the haughtiness gone from her voice.

"And . . .?"

"I saw the ad in a magazine for retired teachers. It looked interesting, so I thought I would apply."

"The fact that it was in a magazine for retired teachers should have been a clue. Twenty-year-olds need not apply."

"I'm not twenty. I'm thirty-two." She was indignant again, but he noticed there was little conviction in her tone. "But if this is about age, I can assure you that I am both mature and responsible."

"I'm sure you are, Ms. Winters." He couldn't very well explain that it most certainly was about age, that he was searching for someone who looked like his grandmother. He walked out from behind the desk and went over to poke the languishing fire. He gave it a vicious jab with the poker, sending a shower of sparks up the chimney. He wanted another Scotch, but he would not pour another. He needed all of his faculties. Already he felt he had missed something important. She had hesitated, and he had failed to discover why.

"I have a lot of experience as well," Chloe said somewhat hopefully from behind him.

"In what?" he said cruelly as he let the poker fall to the stone hearth with a clatter. He leaned back against the mantel. He had definitely rattled her, and he felt his edge returning. He'd get her to come clean yet.

She had been nursing her drink in careful little sips, but now she finished it off in a single swallow and set it on the desk. "How about we start again?" she said.

Gaelan noted she had put her schoolmarm voice back on. Nobody had spoken to him like that since he was ten. Maybe she would make him sit in the corner. He almost smiled at the thought and suddenly realized that maybe he was enjoying this a little too much. No wonder he had let himself get dragged into an argument. "I don't think we need to start again. I've made up my mind—you're going." Did he detect the slightest bit of regret in his own voice?

Perhaps Chloe detected it, too. "I came such a long way," she said quietly, dropping the schoolmarm tone. There was a note of pleading in her voice. She looked at her feet, and her hair fell around her face like a rich curtain.

"I told you I'd compensate you," he said firmly. He could not allow himself to feel regret.

"But I don't want six months' pay for doing nothing. I want to stay here and teach. Even more so, now that I've met Sophia." She looked up and pushed the strawberry-blond waves back from her face. "Has she ever shown you her drawings?"

This was not a conversation that Gaelan was comfortable with, and was part of the reason he had given the job of interviewing to Marcus. How was he to explain that he had virtually nothing to do with the child—that just to look at her brought back her mother and a whole history he would just as soon forget? He felt guilty, of course, and he knew he was being a terrible father, but that's the way it was.

"Sometimes," he said, although it was a lie. Sophia never showed him anything—she knew he didn't like her to bother him. They didn't even eat meals together. Sophia ate in the kitchen with Windy, while Gaelan ate here in his office. And with his business, weeks could go by without them seeing each other at all. Really, her impassioned plea not to send Chloe away tonight was more than she'd said to him in months.

"They're very good, aren't they?"

"I suppose so," he said evasively. He would ask Sophia to show him her drawings tomorrow.

"She's very talented, and I'd like to encourage her to draw more."

Gaelan said nothing, but Chloe was not deterred. "She likes animals too, doesn't she?"

This Gaelan did know. "Yes, she does." She'd asked for a kitten for her sixth birthday, and even he had been touched by her delight when he presented her with the tiny tabby. And on several occasions he had heard her chattering to Windy about the puppy she would like to have.

"I believe in working with a child's interests," Chloe said. "It makes learning much more natural."

Gaelan could see the interest in her eyes, and he had to admit she looked genuinely excited about the prospect of teaching Sophia. Could he be wrong? Maybe Marcus wasn't matchmaking at all. Maybe he was only thinking of Sophia. And God knows, it was good someone was. Gaelan felt her eyes on him and became aware she was waiting for an answer to the question she'd just asked him. "I'm sorry, what did you say?"

"Does she speak any French?" Chloe repeated.

He shook his head. He had put French as a job requirement in his advertisement, believing everyone should know a second language. This being Canada, French was the obvious choice. He himself was completely bilingual but had never spoken French to Sophia. Just another one of the ways he had failed her.

Chloe continued. "I'm fluent in French. My father grew up in Massachusetts, but my mother was born in Quebec City. I thought we could speak French together at least part of the day. Children learn very quickly. Has she started learning the piano? I teach piano as well."

"Nobody is doubting your teaching qualifications, Ms. Winters," he said, feeling annoyed with himself. He wouldn't risk it. He couldn't.

"Chloe," she insisted. "And if it isn't my teaching abilities that are in question, what is?" she asked almost desperately.

"I thought I told you. I was looking for someone who is retired."

"And I thought I addressed that sufficiently," she insisted.

"Not for me." He watched as a lock of hair fell

down over her eye. He felt an urge to reach out and tuck it behind her ear. The thought suddenly made him notice it was getting hot by the fire, so he edged away, a move that unfortunately narrowed the space between them. He forced himself to look away from the tempting lock of hair. He was suddenly aware of how much he was holding himself back. It would be good to feel her body against his. He swallowed hard and hoped the thought didn't reach a certain uncontrollable part of his anatomy. "So unless you can age forty years overnight"—*God forbid*, he thought dryly—"I don't think there's any way for you to satisfy my requirements."

"But—"

"There are no buts," he said firmly. "What are you going to do out here? Widow's Cliff is extremely isolated. Yes, Puffin's Cove is close, but it's hardly a bustling metropolis. And as you know, St. John's is two hours away—in the winter, both places might as well be a million miles away, given the roads can be closed for days on end."

"I don't mind isolation. I love it. I may have lived in Boston, but I like to go camping on the weekends—"

"This is not camping on the weekends. This is all year round. And I do not allow visitors at Widow's Cliff. None. I expect total privacy."

"But surely you allow Sophia's friends to come and visit?" Chloe said, looking taken aback.

"No, I do not. This is my house, and I like it to be quiet."

"But she doesn't go to school. What does she do for friends?"

"Once a week she goes to an enrichment class in Puffin's Cove. That's sufficient." He had no idea whether it was or not, but he couldn't tolerate the thought of noisy children running around the house, and he certainly couldn't let her go to the local school—all he needed was for her to be kidnapped.

"She's just a little girl. She should have friends . . ."

"Look, we're not talking about Sophia, we're talking about you. Sophia is quite used to the quiet here. You are not. This is no place for a young woman from the city. As I said, no visitors are allowed here, so there will be no inviting your boyfriend—"

"I don't have a boyfriend," she interrupted.

"Isn't that a surprise," he said sarcastically, taking this as another indication of her intentions in coming to this lonely place.

"What's that supposed to mean?" she said defensively. "Am I that repulsive?"

Surprised by this answer, Gaelan looked her up and down slowly, his gaze lingering on the rise of her breasts before moving on to her tiny waist and the curve of her hips. "Not at all," he said. He bet Marcus knew this girl didn't have a boyfriend. Who was he trying to kid? Marcus hadn't been interviewing a teacher for Sophia; he had been interviewing a potential wife. Gaelan had told Marcus he was finished with women, but Marcus stubbornly refused to stop trying to set him up. But one thing was for sure about Marcus: he knew what Gaelan found attractive in a woman. He glanced unconsciously at her breasts, feeling an unmistakable hardness forming.

"Oh, I see," she said. "You're afraid I'm going to throw myself at you. That's why you wanted an older woman. You think just because you're rich and attractive . . ." She stopped short on the word *attractive*, and Gaelan felt something akin to pleasure that she found him good-looking. But wasn't this exactly what he wanted to avoid? He was getting confused.

"You think," she repeated, "that just because you're rich, I'm going to throw myself at you? I've never been so insulted!" Gaelan watched her stamp her foot with indignation. He had never heard of anyone doing that outside of a storybook. Rumpelstiltskin, wasn't it? Only Rumpelstiltskin wasn't as cute as Chloe. He found it rather amusing.

"It wouldn't be the first time someone's thrown herself at me," he said sardonically. "And you did call me attractive."

"It's a figure of speech and nothing more," she said angrily.

"A figure of speech," he said slowly. Gaelan may have been out of practice with women lately, but he was pretty sure he had read the signs correctly. The attraction was there, and although he had no intention of getting involved with this beautiful woman, it certainly couldn't hurt to just have a little taste. After all, that's what she'd come for, wasn't it? Certainly, it would prove his theory right or wrong much more quickly than all this talking, he decided, justifying himself and what he was about to do. "I think we'd better test your figure-of-speech theory," he said in a low voice.

He closed the space between them and took her roughly in his arms. The feel of her was astonishing, the skin of her arms warm and soft. He slid his hand around her back, up to the bare skin on her neck, under her thick, soft hair. He bent his head down to hers, seeing his desire reflected in her green eyes. He was right, but he didn't care anymore. Her lips parted as he took her mouth with his. Electricity shot through every nerve ending in his body, filling him with a heart-stopping white heat. It was exhilarating—he couldn't remember ever feeling this before—that the touch of a woman's lips could feel so right. He pulled her closer, crushing her breasts against his chest, his tongue greedily seeking hers.

God, he thought, *don't let this stop. I don't care if this woman was sent by the devil himself. I want her!* All those years of celibacy and denial—this was what he'd been missing! One hand still tangled in her hair, he let his other hand slide down her back to the delicious curve of her buttocks.

Did all this happen in a moment? He didn't know. He didn't care. And so when she shoved her hands against his chest and ripped herself out of his grasp, he didn't know if he'd been kissing her for a minute or an hour. Nor did he know why she had pushed him away; he had felt her mouth hot on his, her lips full and moist.

And when her hand flew up and struck him across the cheek, he was more than just a little surprised.

"What the hell was that for?" he said angrily, his cheek stinging where she had hit him. She had quite the arm on her.

"You have to ask?" She fairly hurled the words at him. Her hair looked wild from where he had tangled his fingers in it, her face was flushed, and her eyes burned. "Of all the arrogant, mean tricks . . ." She hesitated as if she couldn't find words bad enough to describe him.

"Calm down," he said, his voice thick with frustrated desire. "It's not like you weren't enjoying it."

"You bastard!" She almost spat the words at him. "I hope you're happy now, because I quit!"

Gaelan stepped out of her reach as she stomped past him toward the door—he wouldn't put it past her to take another swing at him. She opened the door, and Gaelan was sure she was about to leave when she whirled around and faced him again. *If looks can kill*, he thought, *I think I'm a dead man.*

"One more thing, Gaelan Byrne," she said in a low voice that shook with emotion. "That's a lovely little girl you have, and you are a disgraceful father!"

And as there was nothing he could say in his own defence, he turned away as she left without closing the door behind her.

* * *

CHLOE RAN THROUGH the hall and practically stumbled up the stairway. At the top she hesitated, wondering in her distress if her room was down the hall to her left or right. She forced herself to stop and think before taking the hall to the left. She got to her room and closed the door gratefully behind her.

The lamp beside her bed cast a soft glow over the room. A few embers still survived from the fire that Windy had laid. Chloe went over to it and with a shaking hand stirred them into life with the poker. She caught sight of herself in the mirror. Her hair was dishevelled and her lipstick smudged. She grabbed a tissue from the box on the bedside table and impatiently rubbed the rest of the lipstick from her lips. She ran her fingers through her hair to smooth it down, the memory of his fingers entangled in it fresh and hot in her mind. But there was nothing she could do to take the wild look out of her eyes, remove the flush from her cheeks, or stop her heart from pounding.

She took a couple of logs from the basket in the corner and placed them on the fire before throwing herself onto the loveseat. What had just happened? One moment she had been defending her job, and the next she had been in his arms.

Why had he done that to her? He seemed so sure she was there to wheedle her way into his bed and fortune. *You wouldn't be the first to try*, he'd said to her. Had he hired someone before who had attempted? That would explain his reluctance to hire someone else young. Had he kissed her to test her? If so, she had failed the test. She had hit him all right, but not before she had returned his kisses with a passion that had matched his own.

Really, if it hadn't been for a voice screaming in her head that she was being made a fool of, she would have let it go on forever. Even then it was all she could do to pull herself away and salvage her pride with a slap across the face. And she'd hit him pretty hard, she thought, a slight smile forming at the corner of her lips.

What would have happened if she hadn't slapped him? Would he have eventually pulled away and said *I told you so*? Or would he have taken her to bed to have his fun and tossed her out in the morning? Somehow she guessed it would have been the latter. Surely he hadn't been faking that lust. She remembered his body as he crushed her against himself. No, he most definitely had not been faking.

She couldn't believe she had reacted the way she had. Yes, she found him very attractive. Who wouldn't? He was *tall, dark, and handsome* incarnate. But he was also arrogant and patronizing and clearly an angry soul. For heaven's sake, he had been downright cruel to her. The list of reasons for her to hate him was pretty long for only having known him a few hours. First, he didn't pick her up at the airport—she was sure she had the right date. Then he almost ran over her with his car and didn't offer to drive her the rest of the way to the house. Then he told her she was fired.

At one point she had been sure he knew the boarding

academy had fired her. *Why aren't you teaching at a school*? he'd asked. And she'd lied to him. She hadn't applied for this job because she wanted a change; she'd applied because she'd been forced by circumstances. It didn't mean she didn't want the job or that she couldn't do it, but in the back of her head, she knew he had a right to know. She sensed that he knew she was covering something up, and maybe that was enough to hurt her case. Not that it mattered anymore. She'd quit, and this time tomorrow she'd be knocking on her parents' door on Cape Cod, asking if she could sleep in the guest room.

However, even if he had learned that she'd been let go from the academy, he had no right to speak to her the way he had. But then, what could she expect from someone who could treat his own child with such coldness? In her years as a teacher she had seen parents who were not necessarily good parents, but never had she known someone who had seemed to downright dislike his own child. He didn't even bother to hide it. Imagine telling her to call him Gaelan instead of Daddy!

And yet after all that, she found herself in his arms kissing him like she'd never kissed anyone before. She'd never kissed Shawn that way—not even when she'd thought she loved him. It had just never been that way. Actually, looking back, it was hard to remember why they had ever gotten together in the first place. They both loved the outdoors, whitewater rafting, and camping, but the moment they went indoors, they had nothing in common. Well, they both taught, but Shawn treated it as a job, whereas for Chloe it was a calling. And Shawn didn't even want children. How was it she hadn't figured that out earlier?

And as for sex, well, she sure didn't remember getting this excited. Just thinking about Gaelan's kiss sent blood coursing through her veins. She had only known him for a few hours, and yet she knew he would torment her dreams. She only had to close her eyes to see his dark eyes—eyes so cold one moment and so full of heat and passion the next. It would be the heat and passion she would remember—the mere memory would make her stop breathing and cause her heart to skip a beat. A new longing had taken root in the very centre of her being, and she had this awful feeling it was there to stay for a very long time.

SHE SIGHED, GOT up from the couch, and walked around the room, trying to dispel the image of Gaelan Byrne and his haunting eyes. Maybe she should go look for him, throw herself on his mercy, beg him to let her stay, plead with him to kiss her again and again and again. But she knew she wouldn't. She had more pride than that, not to mention a strong sense of reality. Even if she begged to stay, could she live with him outside the bedroom? Could she bear to see him be so unloving to his daughter? Could she stand it if he were unloving to her? Which was the way it would be. Gaelan had already proved he had few feelings to spare. Sexual feelings maybe, but not emotional.

How had he been with his wife? Was he passionate with her? Did he love her so much that when she died, something died inside him, too? Did he love his daughter then too, but now could not bear that she reminded him of his wife? Maybe that explained his behaviour. Maybe there was a sad story behind the anger. She would never know the answers, because in a few hours she would be gone. She would never see him again.

There was a cautious knock on her door. Chloe stopped her pacing so suddenly she had to grab the back of a chair to keep from falling. Her heart pounded in her chest, and her voice caught in her throat. He had come to look for her! Had he been pacing around his room too, unable to get her out of his mind? She tried to call out—she wanted to tell him to come in. Pride and common sense be damned! She wanted him and she wanted him now—she didn't care if she regretted it the rest of her life. She couldn't leave here without again feeling his mouth on hers. She longed to tangle her fingers in his thick hair. She wanted to undress him, pull him down onto the bed with her, feel his body beside her, inside her . . .

The door opened a crack, and she took a small step toward it, ready to sell her soul to the man behind it if only for one night of happiness.

"It's me, Windy. Are you still awake?" It was the housekeeper. Chloe felt her knees almost buckle under her. She found her voice—a small squeak, all she could manage.

The door opened all the way, and Windy came in carrying a tray with a steaming mug and a bottle of brandy beside it. There was a small covered dish as well. "I heard you pacing in here and decided to bring something from the kitchen to calm you." She placed the tray on a small table at the end of the couch. "It's hot milk and honey. Add a dash of brandy, and I promise you'll sleep like a baby." Windy smiled at her, a comforting sympathetic smile like a mother might give a child. She was wearing a long quilted flannel housecoat in a large floral pattern of pink roses, and for a moment Chloe was reminded of her own mother.

She smiled back weakly and thanked Windy for the tray. "I think I'll add more than a dash of brandy," she said as she poured a generous amount into the milk. She took a sip and agreed that it was indeed soothing.

"I don't mean to pry," Windy said gently, "but I have a feeling your interview with Gaelan didn't go so well."

Afraid of letting her emotions show, Chloe went to the fire and stirred it with the poker. Even then it was hard to control her voice. "I'm leaving in the morning," she said, her voice cracking slightly.

"I know—Gaelan told me. I told him he was making a mistake, but I'm afraid he doesn't listen to me."

"Does he listen to anyone?" Chloe asked bitterly, giving the fire a vicious poke.

"No, I'm afraid not. He's as stubborn as a mule on Sunday. But I can tell you he's a good man under all that stubbornness. I've known him since he was a child."

Chloe replaced the fire screen and turned to face Windy. Could he be so bad if this kind woman was so loyal? "Thank you for being so nice. I wish I could stay and help look after Sophia. I think you're the only person she has."

Windy shook her head sadly. "I know," she said. "The poor little thing needs a mother. And a good one, not like her own mother was."

Chloe was shocked. "Do you mean even her own mother didn't love her?"

Windy looked a little nervous. "I don't think Colleen loved anyone except herself," she said in a bitter rush before catching herself. Chloe had the feeling that Windy regretted her words. No doubt she felt she'd been indiscreet. "It's bad luck to speak ill of the dead," she continued with a finality that implied she would not answer any more questions on the subject.

"Thank you for the milk and brandy," Chloe said, wishing that Windy would tell her more.

"There's some toast as well. I don't know whether you had a chance to eat dinner tonight."

Chloe reflected back over the day. "Except for your cookies, I don't think I've eaten anything since noon." She managed another weak smile. "I think that's been the least of my worries. But thanks. I appreciate your thinking about me, and I'll take the tray down to the kitchen when I've finished."

Windy dismissed her offer with a wave of her hand. "Don't bother. I'll pick it up in the morning." She opened the door and turned to Chloe one last time. "If it were up to me, you wouldn't be leaving tomorrow. I haven't seen Sophia this happy for a long time—and I hate to think how she'll take your departure. She's going to be so disappointed." She shrugged as if there were nothing that could be done. "Good night, Chloe."

"Good night, Windy, and thank you again." The door closed behind the older woman, and Chloe knew it was final. If Windy couldn't make Gaelan change his mind, then it was over. She lifted the cover off the toast. It looked like good homemade bread, but the thought of eating made Chloe feel nauseous, and she hurriedly replaced the lid. She went back to her pacing, sipping the warm milk and brandy, wondering when the mixture would begin to work its magic and make her sleepy.

She had been shocked by Windy's disclosure. Colleen. The name of Gaelan's wife. She had not imagined Sophia's mother had also been unloving. Poor child. But Windy had seemed to imply that Colleen hadn't loved Gaelan either. Was that why he was so bitter? He had married a woman who didn't love him? Windy had said Gaelan was a good man. Could a cruel wife make you bad? Certainly, it might make you very angry. She wondered how Colleen had died. An illness? An accident? How had Gaelan felt when she died? She would never know the answers to these questions, especially since she didn't know the answer to the most important question of all: Had he loved her?

Her mug empty, she put it back on the tray. The brandy was having its effect, if only to make her a little light-headed. She went to her suitcase and dug out a long nightgown, a black lacy one that she loved for its luxurious feel. It was the only thing she owned in pure silk, and it always made her feel sexy and exotic. She decided that tonight she needed the reassurance that she was attractive and desirable. She took off her black dress and folded it neatly before putting it into her suitcase. Then she stripped off the rest of her clothes and let the nightgown slide down over her body.

She looked at herself in the full-length mirror on the back of the bedroom door. Her eyes were no longer flushed and bright, only sad and tired. But she did look good in the negligee, her skin creamy and pale in contrast to its dark sheen. The tops of her breasts were visible over the lace, nipples outlined in black silk. It clung to the narrowness of her waist and flowed over her hips to the floor. She imaged Gaelan's eyes on her and felt a heat surge through her body. She went to the bed and pulled down the covers, ready to get in and face a night of insomnia punctuated by restless dreams, then she remembered Sophia.

She had promised to say good night to Sophia, and although the girl was probably long asleep, it was a promise she would keep. It was the very least she could do for her—she refused to be added to the list of people who had let Sophia down. She pulled the matching silk robe out of her suitcase and slipped it over her shoulders before going down the hall to Sophia's room.

The door was open a crack. A bedside lamp was on, illuminating the girl's face, angelic in sleep as children always are. Chloe opened the door wider and slipped inside. The girl's blond curls fanned out around her face, and Chloe thought the only thing missing was a luminescent halo. Funny that her hair was so blond given how dark Gaelan's was. Perhaps her mother had been blond. It was one more mystery that Chloe would never know the answer to.

In the crook of her arm Sophia held a teddy bear, while curled up beside her on the colourful patchwork quilt was a sleeping tabby cat. A picture book lay open on the covers. Chloe quietly closed it and set it on the bedside table. The cat opened his eyes and regarded her dispassionately for a moment before closing them once again.

The room was big and clearly designed with a child in mind. A fireplace graced one wall, although instead of a real fire, an electric fire with artificial logs cast a warm red glow on the room. On either side of the fireplace sat huge bookcases, the shelves lined with books and toys, and Chloe again had the impression of a poor little rich girl. Did Gaelan think that all these things, as much as any child would want them, could take the place of a parent's love?

She watched the girl as she slept peacefully, feeling a deep sadness. She would be gone in the morning and would never see Sophia again. Perhaps in the long run it was for the best. How could she be this child's teacher for a year and then leave? What effect would that have on Sophia? What Sophia really needed was not a teacher, but a mother who would stay with her forever, to be there as she grew up, to help her through all of childhood and adolescence's ups and downs.

Chloe remembered her own mother, who had comforted her and supported her, no matter what. She recalled her first boyfriend. She was fifteen, and he was eighteen. Her mother hadn't approved and told her so, and yet, when he inevitably dumped her for a cheerleader, her mother had let Chloe cry on her shoulder and never once said *I told you so*.

Chloe couldn't understand Gaelan's lack of affection for the child. Had he always been this angry, or had it been different when his wife was alive? Or had Sophia simply been an unwanted child? But how could anyone not want this beautiful, bright girl? Chloe had only known her for a few hours, and already she was ready to step into the role. Was part of that her attraction to Sophia's father? How would she feel if she heard one day that Gaelan had remarried? Would she be happy for Sophia's sake?

She pulled the quilt up over the girl's shoulders before leaning over and kissing her softly on the cheek. Sophia smiled slightly in her sleep and pressed the teddy bear closer to her chest. "Good night," Chloe said in a barely audible whisper. "I wish I had the chance to get to know you. I do know you are a very special little girl." She straightened up and watched Sophia sleep for a few more moments. What would happen to Sophia? Chloe prayed that despite everything she would grow to be a loving young woman, that her talents would blossom, and that above all, she would be happy. "Goodbye," she whispered again. She turned to leave, then she stopped suddenly, her hand flying to her mouth to stifle a gasp of surprise.

Gaelan Byrne stood in the open doorway of Sophia's room. *How long has he been standing there?* Chloe wondered. His hands were in his pockets, and he lounged casually against the door frame, silently watching her. Despite his closeness, she wondered for a moment whether he was really there or she was dreaming or having a hallucination. But no dream or hallucination could have a presence like this. It was too strong, too physical. All around him the air was charged, his strength and sexuality surrounding him like an aura.

He did not speak; the only movement was his even breathing. That and his eyes. They roamed languidly over her, calmly taking in her appearance in the black silk negligee. She felt almost naked under his gaze and pulled the edges of the robe together over her breasts. Her hand was shaking slightly, and her legs felt so weak that the slightest breeze would have toppled her. She wondered if he would take the few steps that separated them to catch her, and if he did, what would happen next.

She tried to find something to say, but found she was hardly capable of thought, let alone speech. She felt herself being simultaneously pulled in and repulsed by his energy, frozen in space and time, a complete slave to his whims and desires. And so she stood there, separated from him by a few feet of floor, a few feet of air, her fate hanging in the balance as she waited for his next move.

He seemed oblivious to her emotional state, watching

her through narrowed eyes. Slowly he straightened up, his shoulder no longer against the door frame, and as Chloe's heart waited to start beating again, he turned away. Then, without saying a word, without revealing his reasons for being there at all, he disappeared silently down the dark hall.

CHAPTER 3

GAELAN STOOD AT THE EDGE OF THE CLIFF, looking out over the Atlantic Ocean. While the day had dawned relatively clear, a dense white fog was now being carried in on a light wind. Before long it would be, as Newfoundlanders said, as thick as pea soup. Below him the icy water pounded against the rocks in its endless quest to wear the island away.

A hundred yards from shore, two blue-white icebergs made their slow and fateful voyage south. Now two shimmering mountains of ice, the icebergs had once formed part of a glacier in Greenland. Carried by the current, they would continue their journey south until they melted into warmer waters. *Ghosts*, Windy called them, and today, shrouded in fog, they looked especially eerie. Despite their unearthly beauty, Gaelan knew well how deadly they could be. What jutted out of the ocean was only the tip of the iceberg, and relatively easy to avoid. But beneath the dark waves, shelves of deadly ice lay patiently in wait for careless ships.

He loved the icebergs, as he loved everything about

Widow's Cliff—the isolation, the wind, the barren beauty, the ever-present sound of the ocean. He rested a hand against the wooden fence that had guarded the cliff's edge ever since his great-grandfather had wandered off and plunged to his death. Colleen had hated Widow's Cliff for the very reasons Gaelan loved it, and spent as little time here as possible. Perhaps that was why she had failed to ruin the place for him. It felt untouched by her, untainted. Here at Widow's Cliff, he could almost forget the whole sorry business. *Almost* being the operative word, as Sophia's presence was a constant reminder of his foolishness.

The wind lifted his hair and the hem of his long wool coat. It was a cool wind, but it held the promise of spring. The fog was growing steadily denser. He couldn't see the icebergs anymore, though he still felt their nearness. Along the shore was a band of ice, and beyond that he could make out the ice pans, broken pieces of ice washed around by the waves. From these, dozens of ducks scouted the water for fish.

He turned toward the house. Shrouded in fog, it looked straight out of a fairy tale. It was such an unlikely house, with its turrets and its leaded windows—a castle in the New World. Gaelan's great-grandfather had come to Newfoundland, forced out of Ireland by hunger. He had been one of the lucky ones and made a fortune as a shipbuilder. But he was not happy here. He missed the soft green of his homeland and couldn't fall in love with Newfoundland's rocky barrenness. He built his house on this cliff, on the far eastern tip of the continent, as close as he could get to his beloved homeland without stepping into the ocean. Eventually, he had, and Gaelan had always wondered if his fall off the cliff truly had been an accident.

The castle had been passed down through the oldest sons until it came to Gaelan—and he supposed one day it would go to Sophia. There was no chance of a son now. And while he had reservations about her inheriting the house, they had nothing to do with her being female. Times had changed, and, Gaelan believed, for the best—at least where women stood. Regardless, any other child would mean another woman in his life, and he was determined that no matter how hard his body rebelled against his rigidly imposed celibacy, there would never be another.

He looked up then and saw her. Chloe. She appeared from the mist, her strawberry-blond hair floating on the breeze, as ethereal and ghostly as the morning. He felt the memory of her body against his and wondered if he could resist this woman's attraction. Turning away from her, he looked out again over the water, now a swirling wall of white, and forced himself to concentrate on the task at hand.

"The fog is so thick," she said quietly behind him. "When I was in my room, I could still see the icebergs, but now there's nothing but this."

"Yes, it can roll in pretty fast," he said, his voice sounding strangely flat and emotionless to his own ears. He would not let her hear the impact she had on him.

She did not say anything for a moment, but he could feel her presence, the fog wrapping them up together in a white misty blanket until they could barely see each other. "I'm ready to go," she said in an attempt at brightness. "I think it best I leave before Sophia gets up."

"That won't be necessary," he said, addressing the Atlantic Ocean. "You can stay."

He told himself he was doing this for Sophia. He had failed the child in so many ways. Poor kid. It wasn't her fault—but he simply couldn't help it. He felt like a monster sometimes, but he just couldn't let himself feel any affection for her. Instead, he bought her presents, toys, books, her cat, knowing as he presented them that all the toys in the world could not compensate for a father's love. And now he would give her Chloe, another compensation for his lack of affection.

He had watched Chloe with Sophia the night before. Despite having known Sophia for only a couple of hours, Chloe seemed genuinely fond of her. She had tucked her in and kissed her good night. The little things a parent would do, the little things he hadn't done since she was a baby, when he had thought it possible for them to be a family: him, Colleen, and Sophia. But they weren't a family, and he was a failure as a father. And so he would let Chloe stay for Sophia's sake.

But was that really true? Was he only thinking about Sophia? Or was he thinking about himself too? He remembered her black silk negligee, the way it clung to every curve of her body, the glimpse of shadowy cleavage before she pulled the wrap around her. And he had surely been thinking about himself when he grabbed her in his study. Really, afterwards, he had been completely ashamed of himself. He had been less than dignified and rather brutish. He knew he deserved the slap across the face, even if he could still swear she had enjoyed that kiss every bit as much as he had.

He looked down over the cliff, but it was like looking through clouds, and while he could hear the water against the rocks, he could see nothing but white fog. It was as if nothing in the world existed but him and this woman. He could barely see her, but he could feel her presence—so close he only had to turn around and reach out to touch her. His common sense told him this was how it started, a physical attraction, then *bang*! In over your head. He was plunging toward disaster. He knew it, and he knew he should do something to stop it, but he had never felt so powerless in his life.

Suddenly he was aware she had yet to respond to his offer. Not trusting himself to turn toward her, he made it again. "If you still want the job, it's yours. On a three-month trial basis, of course." He would not throw caution completely to the winds.

"I think Sophia will be very happy," she said at last.

"And you?" he asked in a low voice. "Will you be happy?"

"I don't know . . . I did quit . . ."

He felt angry at her hesitation and knew that as much as he was attracted to her, he was far from trusting her.

What would Windy say? *Once burnt, twice shy?* There seemed to be something calculably coy in her indecision, and he felt like she was playing games with him. And he'd had enough games from Colleen to last a lifetime. He turned around to face her, taking a step forward so he was just arm's distance away. "If it's about last night, don't worry. I can assure you it won't happen again."

He had hit a nerve—he could see that in the way she narrowed her eyes and straightened her shoulders. "I should hope not," she snapped back loudly. So loudly that Gaelan decided she was protesting too much. He didn't know whether that pleased him or not.

"So, you'll take the job?" he asked impatiently.

"Yes. I will," she said quietly, and Gaelan tried to read her thoughts. "I'll go and see if Sophia is up yet," she said and turned away.

"Wait," he said, putting a hand on her shoulder to stop her. It was an unconscious gesture, and yet as he pulled his hand away he wondered if he hadn't wanted an excuse to touch her. She turned but stepped away from him, putting distance between them, seeming unsure of what was about to happen next. Did she think he was going to kiss her again, despite what he'd just said?

"I want to make a couple of things absolutely clear," he said firmly. He was serious, he told himself—it was not going to happen again. Not with Chloe, and not with anyone else. "You are here to teach Sophia. I do not want to be bothered. Ever. No parent-teacher interviews, no cute little plays or recitals, nothing."

He noted her look of disapproval but did not acknowledge it. He couldn't bear signs of affection from Sophia; every one of them made him more acutely aware of his own awkwardness in showing affection and warmth for her. Shouldn't he, given the circumstances, feel even more loving toward her? He wanted to. And all of a sudden, he desperately wanted to trust this woman. "The second thing," he continued. "Sophia's mother is dead, and we do not speak about her. I expect you to respect that if ever Sophia should mention her."

Chloe looked as if she was about to protest, but she only nodded. "Is that all?" she asked.

"One other thing. She is forbidden to go anywhere near the cliff, even with adult supervision. More than one person has gone over that edge. Do you think you can handle it?"

"I guess I'll have to." Her hair fell across her eyes, and she pushed it back impatiently. "For Sophia's sake, I'll take the job."

CHLOE FOLLOWED GAELAN back to the house, avoiding the patches of snow that still dotted the ground. She would have liked to have lingered by the cliff to collect her thoughts and enjoy the view, but the fog was now so thick she could barely see the house, and she was not keen on getting lost.

She honestly didn't know how she felt about staying. During the largely sleepless night, she had become so convinced that it was better to leave that now she had to convince herself all over again of why she wanted to stay. *For Sophia's sake*, she would keep reminding herself. The poor child needed someone who cared for her. Her decision, she told herself firmly, had nothing to do with this man whose arrogance and coldness by far made up for his dark, romantic looks. Gaelan Byrne, she decided, made her ex-boyfriend Shawn, even with his refusal to consider children, look downright chivalrous.

They finished the walk in silence. Inside the front door, she picked up her bags and carried them back up to her room. Yet again, Gaelan didn't bother to help. He didn't even seem to notice. His cellphone had rung just then and, talking in a hushed tone, he walked right past her and down the hall that led to his study.

Sophia was not in her room. Chloe found her in the kitchen eating breakfast with Windy. The room was warm and cheerful. A fire burned in the huge fireplace, and the air was fragrant with the smell of woodsmoke, coffee, and home baking. Bunches of herbs hung from the dark ceiling beams, adding their own pungency to the mix. "Chloe!" Sophia shouted, jumping from the table. She launched herself at Chloe and wrapped her arms around her waist. "I don't want you to go!"

Chloe put her arms around the girl's shoulders. "That's good, because I'm here to stay for at least three months."

Sophia let go of Chloe and jumped up and down while clapping her hands. "Windy! Chloe can stay!"

"I heard, dear. It's good news." Windy got up from the table. "But you're going to wear her nerves right raw with all that noise. Sit down and let Chloe have some breakfast."

Sophia sat down obediently and began to shovel big spoonfuls of cereal into her mouth.

"Good heavens, girl!" Windy scolded. "Slow down or you'll choke!"

Sophia responded by eating with exaggerated slowness, moving her spoon very slowly to her mouth. Her joke soon became too much for her though. She started to laugh and almost fulfilled Windy's prophecy. Windy vigorously thumped Sophia on the back until she stopped coughing. "You'll be the death of me, you know. Now behave so I can get Chloe something to eat."

Sophia nodded meekly and ate obediently while Windy brought Chloe a cup of coffee and a couple of muffins still warm from the oven. "Would you like to help me unpack after breakfast, Sophia?" Chloe asked as she spread butter on her muffins.

Sophia nodded and pushed away her empty bowl. "After that can we start school?"

Chloe smiled. "If you like."

"Goody," Sophia said, clapping her hands. "I want to draw on the chalkboard in the schoolroom."

"You have a schoolroom?" Chloe said, but the tabby cat ran under the table and Sophia was right behind it, leaving Windy to answer for her.

"Oh yes, and it's lovely. Gaelan had it done for the last teacher." Windy looked around for Sophia as if worried Sophia might hear. But Sophia was sitting under the table talking to the cat, oblivious to everything else. "She hardly paid any attention at all to Sophia," she continued in a conspiratorial whisper. "She was too busy throwing herself at Gaelan."

Chloe recalled her confrontation with Gaelan the night before. *You think just because you're rich, I'm going to throw myself at you*, she'd said . . . *It wouldn't be the first time*, he'd answered. That had been just before he'd kissed her. She felt the white rush of heat at the memory and bent her head over her coffee, hanging onto the cup with both hands.

"How long was that teacher here?" she asked Windy, forcing her voice to stay calm.

"She was here for two months before Gaelan sent her packing. She was up to no good. The last straw was finding out she was spying for one of those supermarket newspapers."

"Was Sophia upset when she left?" It was important she keep her thoughts focused on her pupil.

"Oh, yes. She cried for days. She just didn't understand." Windy got up from the table and went back to the stove. She lifted a towel from two rising loaves of bread and slid them into the oven. "But I've never seen Sophia take to anyone like she's taken to you. So I don't want to see you leave. The poor girl." She closed the door on the loaves and straightened her back. Then suddenly she looked at Chloe and grinned. "I've known Gaelan for a very long time, and I can't say I've ever seen Gaelan get a bee in his bonnet over anyone like the one he's got in his bonnet over you."

SOPHIA, TRUE TO her word, helped Chloe unpack. She took a critical interest in Chloe's wardrobe and expressed the opinion that someone as pretty as Chloe should have nicer clothes.

"But I like wearing jeans and sweaters," Chloe answered. "They're warm and comfortable. And what about you? You're pretty, but you're wearing jeans and a sweater."

Sophia thought for a moment. "But my sweater is prettier."

Chloe laughed. "Yes, I think you're right. Maybe we can go shopping one day together, and you can help me pick out some pretty sweaters."

Sophia seemed satisfied and put the last of the offending sweaters in the drawer.

Together they carried the few school supplies that Chloe had brought to the schoolroom on the first floor. Chloe had not known what to expect in the way of educational materials and had brought a few books that she was particularly fond of teaching from, including a French primer and a couple of beginner piano books.

She needn't have worried. On seeing the schoolroom,

she came close to tears. It was a teacher's dream come true. Even the well-off private schools in Boston where she'd worked didn't have materials like this. And no classroom could ever have been half this beautiful! The room was twice as large as Chloe's last classroom. A row of windows looking out on the foggy morning graced the length of the room, each windowsill full of cushions perfect for curling up on and reading or dreaming the afternoon away, while tall bookcases groaned under the weight of books.

Sophia skipped to the end of the room and began to draw multicoloured rainbows on the chalkboard. Chloe went to the large antique desk in the centre of the room. It was beautiful, but Chloe felt too authoritarian behind it and knew she would not teach at it. Besides, there were plenty of other places to sit and work, from the cushioned windowsills to the large harvest table that faced the chalkboard. At the far end of the room, a loveseat faced the inevitable fireplace, and a baby grand piano stood before the windows.

It was a beautiful classroom, but as much as Chloe knew how lucky Sophia was to be able to learn in such delightful surroundings, she felt sad when she thought of all the children in overcrowded, sterile rooms with barely enough textbooks to go around.

Feeling overawed, Chloe decided to take her cues from Sophia. "What do you want to learn about on the first day of school?" she said, admiring Sophia's colourful creation on the chalkboard.

"Animals!" Sophia announced without hesitation.

"I thought so," Chloe said. "How about we go to the bookcases and find some books on animals? We can read for a while together, and then we'll learn some animal names in French. How does that sound?"

Sophia agreed, and before long, they were curled up on the couch before a newly laid fire. Chloe wasn't surprised that Sophia already had basic reading skills. She was so bright that she seemed to learn almost by osmosis. She liked both factual books and traditional children's stories. So long as there were animals in the book, Sophia was happy. Sophia read a simplified version of *The Three Billy Goats Gruff* to Chloe, and Chloe read a more difficult story about magical animals, based on Native Canadian legend.

After lunch they put on their coats, and Chloe pushed Sophia on the swing behind the house, but they were soon forced inside by a cold misty rain. It was cozy by the schoolroom fire, and Chloe spread the pieces of a wildlife puzzle across the harvest table. As they put each animal together, Chloe told Sophia the name of the animal in French.

However, as absorbed as Chloe was in her new pupil, she could not help but let her thoughts wander to the child's father. She had not seen him since their early-morning encounter on the cliff, but she continued to feel his presence as keenly as if he were looking over her shoulder. Indeed, the feeling was so strong sometimes that she found herself wanting to turn around to see if he was standing behind her. But she didn't, telling herself she was being paranoid, although it was possibly also wishful thinking.

GAELAN CLOSED THE office door, went to the mantel, and poured himself a drink. He had strict rules about drinking during the day, but today he decided to make an exception.

All morning he had found excuses that took him past the schoolroom door. He would linger there for a moment, listening to Sophia's laughter and Chloe's steady, reassuring voice, carefully pronouncing animal names in French for Sophia to repeat. It was obvious that Sophia was happier than she had been in months, and while he could find no fault with Chloe's teaching style, he still found himself hanging around the door.

But assessing Chloe's pedagogical abilities wasn't the only reason he couldn't stay away. He took a sip of his Scotch. *How do you begin to trust again? Put the past behind you and move on?* He pictured their fair heads close together as they leaned over the jigsaw puzzle. How he longed to be able to say, *I trust you. You are not like Colleen or the other women who pretended to care for Sophia but who were really only interested in my money.*

He went over to his desk and sat down. Two envelopes, delivered that afternoon by courier, sat in the middle of the desk. The first envelope concerned some of Byrne

Enterprises' latest investments. He read it quickly and set it aside. Routine stuff, nothing Marcus couldn't handle.

The other envelope was from a private detective firm he had hired to run a background check on Chloe. Funny, he'd forgotten he'd ordered one. It had been a bit of an afterthought, but after the last teacher, he'd thought it couldn't hurt. He shuddered in distaste as he remembered how that teacher had come into his room at night and, before he could tell her to leave, had opened her robe and revealed her naked body to him. He thought the file had arrived a bit late, then he remembered that Chloe wasn't actually supposed to start until the following week.

He pulled the file out of the envelope and set it on his desk. The first item was an eight-by-ten glossy photo of Chloe. It had been taken on the steps of a red brick building. Her apartment? It was obvious that Chloe didn't know she was being photographed. She was looking not toward the camera but into the distance, as if wondering about her next course of action.

Gaelan felt two things as he looked at the picture. First, that tug of attraction. The thoughtful eyes, the hair that only moments ago he had wanted to smooth, and the mouth—her lips slightly parted and so absolutely kissable. But soon attraction gave way to guilt. He told himself he had every right to check into her past—not only because of the last teacher and her lust for his money, but also for Sophia's protection and safety.

He set the photo aside, picked up the report, and read it. He slammed it on the desk less than ten minutes later. He got up and went down the hall to the schoolroom, knocking sharply on the already open door.

Chloe and Sophia were standing at the table, admiring the completed puzzle. Both looked up, startled by the sudden noise. It was Sophia who recovered first. "Come and see the puzzle, Daddy . . . I mean Gaelan," she exclaimed. "I know all the animals in French, too." She pointed to an elephant in the puzzle. "This is *un elephant—*"

"That's very nice, Sophia," Gaelan said, interrupting her sharply. "But I don't have time for that now. I need to speak to Chloe. Go and stay with Windy in the kitchen."

"But we still have school," Sophia protested. Her face, that had looked so happy moments ago, now crumpled with disappointment.

Damn! I've done it again, Gaelan thought guiltily. All he ever did was make the kid feel bad. It was just that he was so furious . . .

He caught Chloe's glare as she put her hands on Sophia's shoulders. "I think we've learned a lot for our first day," Chloe said gently. "How about we call it quits for today? We'll do lots of new things tomorrow." She glanced his way again, and Gaelan could see she was worried there might not be a tomorrow. *And for good reason*, he thought.

Sophia conceded reluctantly. She gave Gaelan a defiant stare as she strode past him, but Gaelan's head was so full of what he'd read in the file on the desk that he barely noticed. With Chloe following, Gaelan turned and walked back to his office, telling her to close the door behind her.

"What's this about?" she demanded. Gaelan knew she was angry he had interrupted her class.

"I think you already know," he said coldly. "Did you think I'd never find out?" He went behind his desk and held out the folder to her.

She stood facing him across the desk. "What's this?" she asked, taking it.

"Open it." he said. He watched Chloe's face as she opened the folder. The photograph slipped to the floor. She put the folder down and leaned over to pick up the picture. Straightening up, she looked at the image of herself and then at him with a puzzled expression on her face.

"Where did you get this?" she asked.

"A private detective. I had a background check done on you."

Puzzlement turned to anger, and she glared at him with the same intensity of dislike as Sophia had only a few minutes before.

"You did what?" she exclaimed. "You spied on me?" Her green eyes flashed fire at him. "How could you do this? How long was this guy creeping around the shrubs waiting to take my picture?" she continued, shaking the picture at him across the desk. "Did he follow me, too?"

Gaelan didn't answer, and she threw the picture at him. "Of all the low-down, sneaky things to do!"

The picture fell face up on the desk in front of Gaelan. "Don't take that self-righteous tone with me," he said heatedly. "It would seem you've been pretty low-down and sneaky yourself." He pushed the picture away and pointed to the open file in front of him. "Why didn't you tell Marcus you were fired from your last job?"

CHAPTER 4

THEY FACED OFF ACROSS THE DESK, BUT whereas a moment ago, Chloe had been staring daggers at him, her eyes now wavered. Gaelan could tell she felt guilty. He recalled their first conversation and how he had thought she was keeping something from him. No doubt this was it. "Well, why didn't you?"

"Because it didn't come up," she snapped back at him, suddenly defiant again.

"It didn't come up," he said slowly. "Just what did you do for a reference?"

"Marcus didn't ask for one. Although I can assure you I had a good one from my previous job."

It was Gaelan's turn to hesitate. Marcus may have wanted to do some matchmaking, but surely he would still have done the bare minimum of making sure this woman was qualified for the job.

"Besides," Chloe continued, "it had nothing to do with my teaching skills."

"According to this, it says you were fired for incompetence."

"Incompetence?" Chloe said in surprise. She grabbed the file from the desk. "Where did you get that from?"

"My detective had an enlightening chat with your boyfriend, Shawn." This deception bothered him more than her being fired. Why would she pretend not to have a boyfriend unless she had hopes of putting the moves on him? And, damn it, he was disappointed—just when he'd thought he could start to trust someone. "I thought you told me you didn't have a boyfriend."

Chloe looked up from the file. "I don't. He's my ex-boyfriend," she said firmly. Then she started to laugh. "I guess your private detective isn't so smart after all."

"Then why don't you tell me the real story?" Gaelan said slowly.

"I'm not sure it's any of your business," she said haughtily.

"It is if you want to keep your job," he answered.

"You seem determined that I should quit this job every day," she said, to his surprise. "I don't know what my personal life has to do with my job."

"Then tell me about your professional life. That, surely, I have a right to know about." He could see her hesitate.

"Fine," she said, her mind clearly made up. "I was almost finished with my master's in education at Boston College, but I had to drop out when I lost my job at a private school due to the recession. I was desperate to make ends meet. When I saw the job opening at the boarding academy, I knew I was qualified even though I didn't quite have the required degree. I must admit that I did technically lie on my resumé, but I was planning to go back and finish the degree as soon as I had earned a few paycheques. When I split up with Shawn, he got his revenge by telling them the truth, and so I was fired." She threw the file back on the desk. "That was it. End of story. It was stupid of me, I know, but perhaps next time, your detectives should go to the source instead of talking to a bitter ex-boyfriend."

Gaelan looked at her and wondered if he'd let his paranoia get the better of him this time. She could be telling him the truth, but he wouldn't know that for sure until he made some inquiries of his own in the morning. He was confused now. He didn't know whether to apologize or fire her.

She seemed to be reading his thoughts. "So, are you going to fire me again? Or am I going to quit? Or am I just going to go eat my dinner and pretend this didn't happen?"

"Go eat your dinner," Gaelan said. He walked around the desk to the door and opened it for her.

She didn't leave immediately but stood only inches from him, looking up at him with those defiant green eyes. "I don't know what happened to you, but you should learn not to be quite so suspicious. It must be a pretty lonely existence."

He didn't know if he was filled with such mixed emotions because she had hit the proverbial nail on the head or because she was standing so very close to him.

Did he want to fire her or kiss her? "I think it's my turn to say it's none of your business," he said at last, and he went back to his desk and picked up the phone.

The next morning Gaelan left for Boston. He didn't tell Chloe he was leaving; she had to hear it from Windy. She couldn't help but think it was to further check up on her, and she imagined teams of detectives now interviewing everyone she'd ever known.

The day was a tense one, with her wondering if, on his return, he would change his mind yet again, and she found herself regretting being so outspoken the night before. The sense of impending doom wasn't helped by the teeming rain that streamed down the classroom windows and kept her and Sophia inside. But as there was nothing to do but carry on until she knew more, she used the time to determine her new pupil's strengths and weaknesses (heavy on strengths and short on weaknesses), as well as her math and reading levels.

At 3 o'clock, she took Sophia down to the kitchen for Windy to watch. On the way back to her room, she paused outside Gaelan's office. That morning, when the two local girls had been in to clean, the door had been open, and she'd put her head in briefly to see one polishing the desk and the other dusting the mantelpiece. Now, she put her hand on the door handle and, feeling guilty, turned it. It was locked. She climbed the stairs and, instead of turning left to her own room, she turned right. The door to his room was at the end of the hall, and, again feeling guilty, she tried the handle. This door, too, was locked, and she turned back and went down the hall to her own room with no idea what she would have done had she found either of them open—she certainly wouldn't have gone snooping. And while she feared what his return might bring, she knew the house felt empty without him.

He came home late the next day. She walked by the office, expecting it be closed and locked as before, but the door stood open, and there he was at the window, his back to her. He must have come straight to his office, as his long black coat was draped over his desk chair and his black gloves were on top of his closed laptop. She stood there wondering whether to speak, both fearing and hoping he would turn around.

A moment later, he did turn. He did not see her immediately, his gaze settling on the fire already crackling on the hearth. He ran his fingers through his thick black hair. In this unguarded instant, there was a vulnerability and sadness in his dark eyes, and Chloe felt as if she was eavesdropping on a profoundly private moment. She would have to either leave or say something, but before she could decide what course of action to take, he saw her.

"How long have you been standing there?" The distrust was back in his eyes, the hand he had been running through his hair now clenched at his side. Even if he did start to trust her, would that trust ever be secure? It took so little for him to become suspicious again. She felt that he was constantly waiting for her to make some slip-up that would prove his suspicions were grounded.

"Only a moment," she said. "I was surprised to see the door open. I didn't know you were back."

"Why didn't you say anything?"

"I didn't want to disturb you."

He didn't respond. Remembering how the last thing he'd said to her before leaving was that it was none of her business, she added cautiously, "Did you have a good trip?"

"I accomplished what I set out to do." There was a pause, and then he said, "Are you getting settled in okay?"

She nodded. "Yes." If he'd done any more investigating of her past in Boston, it would seem that it had satisfied him. *Are you getting settled in okay?* didn't seem to be a prelude to another firing. Maybe she could relax. She wondered for a moment if he might ask her in, if he might even offer her a drink, her eyes now roaming to his shirt open at his throat, the top two buttons already undone . . . She suddenly felt she had to apologize for their last meeting. "I'm sorry—"

"Good," he said, cutting her off, his no-nonsense tone intruding on the fantasy already forming in her head. "And now, if you'll excuse me, I still have work to do. Would you mind closing the door for me?"

She did as requested, standing there for a moment, trying to remember where she'd been going when she'd seen the open door. In the end, she turned around, went back into the hall, and took the stairs up to her room, knowing full well she'd been going nowhere other than to find out if he was back.

Once in her room, she undressed and put on the flannel pyjamas she'd brought, remembering how that first night she'd worn the black silk nightgown. Tonight had seemed to tell her a few things. First, for some reason, he'd decided to trust her enough to let her stay. But she knew, too, this was a fragile trust—she had seen the transition in his face the moment he noticed her standing there. It wouldn't take much for him to distrust her again. He would never see her desire for him as anything but a desire for his wealth. If she were going to stay here, she would have to accept this was an employer-employee relationship only. Or, in the case of Gaelan, with his dark, sexy, romantic looks and commanding presence, more like lord and servant. Would there ever come a day when the sight of him didn't result in her heart rate quickening or in some erotic dream or fantasy? She looked at herself in the mirror in her sexless blue flannel pyjamas dotted with pink hearts. "This is the way it is, Chloe Winters. Get over it."

It was of course, easier said than done, but over the next week, she started to settle into the routine that would be the rhythm of her life at Widow's Cliff.

By 7 a.m., one of Windy's local girls would leave a tray with coffee and breakfast outside her door. She would then eat, bathe, and dress. At 9 a.m., she'd meet Sophia in the classroom. Reading, spelling, recess, then arithmetic until noon. They would eat lunch together in the kitchen and return to the classroom for French, music, and drawing. At 3 p.m., she would take Sophia to the kitchen, where she had a snack and played under Windy's supervision until suppertime. The rest of the afternoon and evening Chloe had to herself. The only discernible break she saw in this pattern was to take Sophia into town on Fridays for her enrichment class and outside for recess—if the rain ever ended.

She did see Gaelan from time to time. They would pass in the hall, and though his eyes stayed guarded, he would even be pleasant. "I'm sorry about the weather. You must think the sun never shines here." And she would be pleasant in return. *Employer-employee*, she'd remind herself. *Nothing more.*

She took to going into the classroom for an hour every night after Sophia was in bed to play the piano. She was not especially talented or accomplished, but she'd learned to play a few things well. The simpler Beethoven sonatas, some Chopin waltzes.

It was during one of these sessions that he did stop and look in. "Very nice," he said. "It's good to hear it played. I'm glad you'll be teaching Sophia." She started to thank him, but he closed the door and moved on, and she was left with an sense of utter aloneness.

She kept to her side of the bargain by not bothering him with anything regarding Sophia, even when the child's cold returned just in time for her Friday enrichment class. Sophia tried to downplay it, saying she was just fine to go into Puffin's Cove. Chloe, too, had been looking forward to it—a break from the strange tensions of living in the same house as a man you were deeply attracted to but couldn't have—but really felt it best not to take chances.

Sophia even went so far as to argue with her, and Chloe was surprised when she looked up to see Gaelan in the classroom door. "Chloe's right, Sophia. It's better you stay home. Perhaps you can have a friend visit next week while I'm away. In the meantime, why don't you watch a movie? That'll be a nice change."

Sophia wasn't too interested in the movie, but she did like the idea of having a friend over, and Chloe felt this must be progress on his part, even if it was while he was away. Maybe underneath all that anger and hurt, there was a good man, as Windy had said. Maybe even she herself was starting to see glimpses of it. But while it was good for Sophia's sake, it just made it all the harder for Chloe. Better he stay angry with her all the time— these glimpses of goodness only weakened her resolve to accept their relationship as only professional.

She saw him again that very evening when he came by the classroom while she was playing piano. "I trust you had no further difficulties with Sophia today," he said.

"No, she seemed very pleased at the prospect of having a friend over," she said. "So, you're going away again."

"Monday. I'll be gone for at least ten days. Good night." He closed the door behind him.

She went back to playing, self-consciously now, as if he might be listening outside. *Gone for ten days*, she thought. *It will feel like a year, and yet this . . . what does this feel like?* She suddenly saw herself here years from now. Sophia growing up, marrying, having her own children, getting dear old Chloe to help, Chloe taking the place of Windy as the servant . . . and even then hoping the aging but still handsome Gaelan would notice and trust her . . .

The weekend passed, and on Monday, the day Gaelan was to leave for ten days, it finally stopped raining, and Chloe was more than happy to interrupt the school day with a long walk along the cliff.

Bearing in mind what Gaelan had said about Sophia going near the fence, Chloe walked hand in hand with Sophia. While the rain had let up, it was still cold, and the wind coming from the north nipped at their cheeks until they glowed bright red. There were no trees along the ridge and no shelter, so they felt the elements full force. Now an occasional flake of snow drifted on the wind, and it seemed that the day could not decide what it wished to do. They walked down into a hollow a little out of the wind, and Sophia pointed out a bird flying out over the ocean in pursuit of a gull.

"What is it?" Chloe asked.

"A peregrine. It's after that gull." They watched as the bird of prey dove repeatedly at the gull, each dive resulting in a narrow miss. Some bigger gulls came to the aid of their comrade, launching their own attacks against the now outnumbered peregrine. The peregrine made a few more attacks on the smaller bird before finally giving up and flying back toward the shore. Chloe knew the peregrine had just been outwitted out of its breakfast, but she breathed a sigh of relief on behalf of the gull, all the same.

"Now look," Sophia said, this time pointing inland. "A bald eagle!" Chloe watched the almost mythical bird as it soared above them, the wind under its wings.

"You know a lot about birds too, I see," Chloe said, impressed with the girl's knowledge.

"Windy taught me, and I put seed on the bird feeders outside the kitchen window. My favourites are the chickadees. I'm going to be an ornithologist when I grow up."

"That's a very big word for such a little girl. Do you know the song about chickadees?"

Sophia shook her head, so Chloe sang it for her. Sophia caught on to the simple little song quickly and soon was singing along happily as they walked up the other side of the hollow, the eagle soaring above their heads, their voices melting into the cold wind.

Just then, a loud crack shattered the air. It came from close by, and even over the sound of the wind and the ocean, it was terrifying in its sudden loudness. Sophia screamed, and Chloe instinctively grabbed her tight. Sophia's scream was followed by another: the eerie, tragic sound of something in pain.

Chloe looked up in horror to see the magnificent eagle faltering in its flight. Sophia had her face pressed into Chloe's coat, and Chloe held her there, not wanting her to see the fate of the falling bird. Sophia began to sob, and Chloe stroked her hair, trying to find a way to tell her what was happening.

At the same time, she looked for the killer. There was no way the shot could have come from the direction of the water; the ocean, choked with broken pans of ice, was unnavigable. There would be no boats out there for a long time. She looked behind her along the length of the headland and the crooked line of the fence but saw nothing. She turned her eyes inland just in time to see a figure rise from behind a boulder in a small copse of stunted trees. She could not see any features from this distance but assumed from the size and clothing that it was a man. He wore a bright orange hunting cap with a dark jacket and pants. His gun was still raised toward the sky, his eye on the floundering bird, as if he were about to fire again and finish off the job.

Chloe screamed at the man to stop, trying to make herself heard over the sound of the wind. She must have succeeded, because he turned and looked to where she stood at the edge of the hollow with Sophia clutching at her coat. Seemingly surprised that anyone else was out on the cold headlands, he brought the gun quickly down to his side. He took one last glance at the sky, turned, and ran away from the cliffs in the direction of the road.

Chloe turned her attention upwards and watched with sick apprehension as the bird continued to lose altitude. Again it cried and flapped its wings as if hoping to stop its plunge to the earth. Chloe prayed that the winds would carry it to the ground. If only it could land without being killed . . . If only the shot weren't fatal . . . If only it didn't land in the ocean where there was no hope of getting to it . . . Perhaps they could save the poor creature.

Chloe became aware that Sophia had dared to take her head out of Chloe's coat. "What happened?" she cried, her voice trembling uncontrollably. "Who were you yelling at?" Sophia's face was streaked with tears, her eyes wide with terror.

Chloe had to be honest with her. She could not see any way of protecting her from what had happened. She pulled a tissue from her pocket and wiped the tears gently from Sophia's face while she gathered the courage to tell her the awful news. She hated when children had to learn about the cruelty of adults.

"A man shot the eagle, and then he ran away." She pointed up to where the bird thrashed in the air.

Sophia looked up and, seeing the bird, let out a terrible cry of anguish. "We have to save it!" she cried.

"I don't know if we can," Chloe said, "but we'll try. I just hope it doesn't fall in the ocean."

"It's going that way," Sophia said, pointing along the edge of the cliff ahead of them. She pulled Chloe by the hand, and they hurried along the cliff, relieved that the bird was moving inland. The bird was now only about thirty feet in the air, still desperately flapping, and Chloe began to wonder if its goal was not to gain altitude but simply to slow its descent. Perhaps there was still hope.

They were now within yards of the bird, and Chloe stopped Sophia. "Let's not scare it," she said quietly. "Let's wait until it lands."

"Okay," Sophia said, her voice little above a whisper. They stood watching as the bird tumbled the last few feet, landing with a dull, painful thud. As Chloe and Sophia cautiously approached, the bird tried to stumble to its feet. Chloe could see blood streaking its side and one wing extended awkwardly from its body. It watched their approach warily, its black eyes under the white hood of feathers fixed on them with suspicion. "It's okay," Sophia cooed softly. "We're going to help you."

Sophia's voice seemed to calm the bird, and it stopped struggling. Instead it drew its wings against its heaving sides, rolled onto its side, and looked at them as if to say, *I trust you.* But despite this seeming show of trust, Chloe approached the bird with caution, afraid it might lash out at her with its large curved beak or sharp talons.

"I'm going to wrap my coat around it and carry it back to the house. We'll have to take it to a veterinarian immediately."

"Will it live?" Sophia asked in a hushed tone.

"I don't know," Chloe answered honestly as she removed her coat, the cold wind instantly penetrating her sweater in icy gusts. "I hope so." Carefully, she placed her coat over the bird's back and neck. It didn't move. Very slowly, Chloe lifted it and finished wrapping her coat around its sharp claws. She held it against her, finding it to be more awkward than heavy. The bird stayed quiet, the only movement its laboured breathing. Chloe knew the bird was in critical condition. "Go tell Windy what happened, and tell her to get a car ready. We have to get it to the vet quick!"

"But Windy doesn't drive," Sophia protested.

Chloe hesitated, Gaelan's words echoing in her mind. *I do not want to be bothered* . . . But she had no choice, and she could only hope his anger at the hunter would trump his annoyance at being interrupted. "Ask Windy to get Gaelan then," she said firmly.

Sophia looked like she had a moment's hesitation as well, but a glance at the bird seemed to give her courage, and she took off in a run toward the house.

UNABLE TO CONCENTRATE, Gaelan put down his pen and went to the window. Windy had brought his lunch in on a tray, but except for the coffee, it sat cold and untouched. He scanned the cliffs, but Chloe and Sophia were nowhere in sight. Windy had told him they were going out for a walk when she brought him his lunch.

Between his meetings in Boston, he had made the necessary calls, and they supported Chloe's story. He was to leave for Montreal for ten days and yet he found himself wanting to stay. He could no longer deny it was due to Chloe. He wondered now if he could start trusting her and let himself explore his feelings for her. He so wanted to—and yet every time he saw her, he felt the old plates of armour snap into place, heard the coldness in his voice even when he was doing his best to be pleasant. He couldn't shake the feeling of distrust. It was like he was looking for something definitive, and yet he didn't know if he would recognize it if he saw it.

Just then, he saw Sophia come tearing along the cliff, her hair flying out behind her. She stumbled and almost fell but did not moderate her breakneck pace. Gaelan could see this was not a game. She was not running for fun. Something was wrong. He scanned the cliffs. There was no sign of Chloe, and Gaelan felt a cold clutch of fear at his heart. Had she been hurt? Where was she? Not the cliff! How many times had he told her?

Quickly shrugging on his coat, he ran out of the house using the door that faced the cliffs. He rushed out to meet Sophia, and she came straight into his arms. He held the girl tightly and looked into her terrified eyes. "Are you okay? Where's Chloe?"

Sophia was so winded and frightened she could hardly speak and, wrenching herself away from Gaelan, pointed down the fenceline in the direction she had just arrived from.

"Is Chloe hurt?" he demanded. Where the hell was she? He imagined her at the foot of the cliffs, her body smashed against the rocks.

"Get the car!" Sophia finally gasped. "We gotta get the car!"

Gaelan tried to interpret Sophia's words. Did Chloe need the car to get to the hospital?

"Show me where she is, Sophia!" he barked, and started to run along the cliff as Sophia struggled to keep up. Just as he was about to scoop her into his arms, he saw Chloe emerge from a hollow in the headland. He stopped and watched her, a sense of relief flooding through him.

He soon noticed she was coatless and carrying a large bundle in front of her. He stopped and watched her approach. "What's that Chloe's holding?" he asked Sophia.

"It's a bald eagle," she said, finally regaining her breath. "A man shot it."

Now Gaelan was angry. Really angry. "Christ," he swore, not caring that Sophia heard him.

"We have to get the car. It has to go to the vet!"

Lifting Sophia, Gaelan strode across the headland and, without saying a thing to Chloe, put down Sophia and took the bird out of Chloe's arms. He laid it on the ground and unwrapped the coat.

The bird had been shot all right, and looking at it, so close to death, Gaelan felt almost blinded by fury. How could anyone possibly justify killing a bald eagle? Not only was it a magnificent animal, the entire species had only recently made it back from the brink of extinction.

"Take Sophia back to the house," he ordered Chloe, wrapping up the bird again and lifting its near-still body in his arms. "I'm going to take the bird to the vet."

"I want to come too!" Sophia cried, clearly close to tears.

"No, Sophia," he said sternly. "Go with Chloe."

"Actually, I'd like to come," Chloe said. "Sophia will be all right with Windy."

Gaelan thought about refusing, but seeing the determined look in Chloe's eyes made him change his mind. "Okay," he finally said. "Meet me at the car. And hurry!"

As he strode to the garage for his car, he saw Chloe lean down and comfort the girl. He swore again. He could have done that. It wouldn't have hurt just to say a few reassuring words to the poor child, so obviously upset. But as usual, he seemed incapable of expressing anything other than impatience with her. It was just that he was incensed over the bird, as well. And then, of course, there was the scare he had had when he thought it was Chloe who was hurt. Funny, he had been so afraid she'd been injured, and yet when he'd found out she was fine, he hadn't say a single word to her.

Once in the car, the bird lying still on the seat beside him, he phoned the veterinarian in Puffin's Cove. The vet expressed his dismay and said he would be ready when they arrived. When Chloe slid into the front seat wearing one of Windy's old coats, Gaelan had her call the police and the game warden to give them a description.

When Gaelan and Chloe finally arrived with the bird, the vet was not hopeful about its chances, but as he hooked up an intravenous, he told them he'd remove the bullet and stop the bleeding. All they could do after that was hope for the best. He told them to call back in a few hours.

On their way out of the veterinary clinic, Chloe surprised him by announcing, "I could use a drink."

"Not a bad idea," he said. "It's hard to return to normal after something like this. I'll take you to the Stinky Cod. Get in the car. Consider it part of the tour package."

She smiled uncertainly at him, and he remembered the incredible relief he'd felt as he saw her come up the rise with the bird under her arm. Yes, he was getting to like the idea of seeing that smile more often. That made him remember he was supposed to be on his plane right now. He pulled out his cell and, excusing himself, called his pilot and then Marcus, telling him something had come up. He would call again later to get the results of the meeting and fly out the next evening.

He was putting his cell away when Chloe asked him if he could call Windy too. "Sophia must be so worried, and at least we can say the bird is at the vet's."

"Of course," he said. Here she was, thinking of Sophia for him again. He was relieved to hear from Windy that the girl was no longer crying but waiting stoically for the outcome. He promised to call her as soon as they heard anything.

"I'm glad Windy's with Sophia. She's such a kind soul," Chloe said as he started the car. "I know that sounds kind of hokey, but she is. How long has she been with you?"

"She looked after me when I was a child, and when Sophia was born, she was more than happy to return. I thought she would've told you all this by now. She certainly loves to talk."

"Yes, but she's also very discreet."

"Is that your schoolmarm way of saying she hasn't let you in on the family skeletons? Our closets are full of them, you know."

"No," she said, clearly feeling awkward. "She hasn't told me anything."

"Nothing about my wife?"

Chloe looked uncomfortable. "Only that you were badly hurt—" She stopped abruptly. "Look, if you don't want to have a drink with me . . ."

He didn't want to continue this way. But old habits died hard. He felt himself wanting to fall for this woman, and yet it took almost nothing for him to become suspicious. But one thing was certain: he really did want to have a drink with her. *Start there, Gaelan*, he told himself. "I'm sorry," he said. "I really do want to have that drink with you. And yes, Windy is a good soul. And yes, my relationship with Sophia's mother was not the happiest. And I can behave like a cad, I know. Maybe I should be asking you if you still want to have that drink with me?"

She nodded. "Yes. And maybe you can tell me about the environmentalism you're active in. Is that a safe topic?"

"It can still get me pretty angry," he said, parallel parking in front of the bar.

"It can make me angry too," she said. "So at least we'll be angry at something other than each other."

He laughed, and his emotions tilted him back toward trusting her again. Walking toward the bar, it was all he could do not to put an arm around her shoulders. He held the door for her and was barely inside it before a round of *Hiya, Gaelan* rang out.

Gaelan was fond of the Stinky Cod Pub. The owner was a burly American named John who had fallen in love with Newfoundland after a vacation to the province twenty years earlier. He'd bought the bar when it was a bankrupt fish market and never tired of telling tourists how when he bought it, it did indeed stink of fish.

It was too early in the season for tourists, and the few patrons were locals. "Looks like we're going to have some weather," they said to Gaelan. The pub was decorated to appeal to the tourists, and the walls were hung with fishing nets, lobster traps, mounted fish, and old advertising signs. But despite the kitschy decor, it was still a favourite of the locals, and the same people were likely to be sitting in it on any given day.

Gaelan held out a chair at a table near the door. John looked up from wiping the bar. "Look at that, it's Gaelan Byrne, the Dark Lord of the Manor himself. And you're out in the daylight. Damn. I had twenty bucks riding on you being a vampire." He laughed. "Now what can I get you two?" he asked even as he pulled from the shelf the single-malt Scotch he kept in stock especially for Gaelan.

"Make it two," Gaelan said as he turned questioningly to Chloe. She nodded, and John smiled at her as he poured two generous shots and put the bottle on the table next to their glasses.

"Chloe, John. John, Chloe."

"Pleased to meet you," Chloe said.

John wiped his hand on his apron. "Not from around here." It wasn't a question.

"Boston."

"Ya, I'm from down that way. Can't remember off-hand where now. You'll feel the same way soon. You been screeched in yet?"

"No. What's that?"

"I'll let Gaelan explain," he said with a wink and went back to the kitchen.

"Do I want to know?" Chloe asked Gaelan.

"It has to do with a bottle of really strong rum called screech and kissing a cod."

"A fish?"

"A fish. It'll make an honorary Newfoundlander out of you." He could barely suppress a smile.

"And there's no other way?"

"Once you drink enough screech, kissing a fish seems quite natural." He was enjoying himself now. "But there's more to it. After you kiss the cod, you must answer the phrase 'Is ye an honorary Newfoundlander?' with 'Deed I is me ol' cock, and long may your big jib draw.'"

"Deed I is me ol' cock . . . what?" she asked, laughing.

"Hey Gaelan! What's the joke?" Gaelan looked up to see Seamus coming toward him, his unlit pipe in his hand. Gaelan had never seen the pipe lit, and he assumed Seamus carried it for the sake of the tourists. With his red beard and the pipe clenched between his teeth, he made a postcard-perfect Newfoundland fisherman.

"Hi, Seamus. Just telling Chloe about getting screech-ed in."

"Not on this girly stuff," Seamus said, picking up the bottle of Scotch and looking at the label. "You're Sophia's new teacher, right?"

She nodded.

"Thought so. Was talking to Windy's nephew. News travels fast here."

"How's Kelly making out?" Gaelan asked before Seamus starting asking too many questions he wasn't prepared to answer yet.

"Fine," Seamus replied. "Just finishing up her exams. She's got her eye on the old general store for her practice. She told me you have to cut the ribbon for the opening."

"I'll be at her graduation with a huge bouquet of flowers." Gaelan turned to Chloe. "Seamus's daughter is going to be a doctor."

"Yup, thanks to Gaelan here." Seamus started doing up the buttons on his jacket. "Gaelan established a scholarship for the high school kids around here a few years back. A full ride to study pre-med at Memorial University. My daughter was the first one to get it, and now she's going to be a doctor. Dr. Kelly Tucker."

"Congratulations," Chloe said. "That's quite an achievement. You have a right to be proud."

"Sure do. Sure could use the doctors around here too. Gaelan has it all planned out. He wants to have local kids setting up medical practices throughout Newfoundland."

"Okay. Enough," Gaelan said. "Just trying to do my bit. Everyone here does."

He tried to sound dismissive, but Gaelan could see Chloe looked impressed. *Damn.* He felt like he was showing off. Like the time when he was six and climbed a tree to impress a girl named Mary. He'd fallen out and started crying. She'd grown up and married Seamus. Probably told him every night how glad she was to have married him instead of that crybaby Gaelan Byrne—even if he was a billionaire.

Seamus was pulling his fur-lined cap down over his ears. "Put a glass of screech on my tab for this girl!" he called out to John behind the bar.

"Give my best to Mary," Gaelan said. "And wish Kelly luck from me for her exams."

"Will do. Nice to meet you, Chloe," Seamus said. He slapped Gaelan once more on the shoulder before opening up the door and letting in a brief blast of cold air.

"I can't believe you set up those scholarships." She sounded kind of incredulous.

Why? Because I seem like such a bad guy? But then he hadn't given her much reason to believe otherwise. "Seamus is a good man," was all he said in the end. "As are all the people in Puffin's Cove. And they like their privacy as much as I do." John came over with the glass of screech, and Gaelan waited for him to set it down in front of Chloe before resuming. "They've got an eagle eye for the paparazzi too. A bunch of them will keep them busy with some ridiculous made-up story while someone else gives me the heads up. Those low-lifes usually end up leaving town feeling pretty stupid. Now let me see you drink that."

She was still wrinkling her nose at the screech when two men entering on a blast of air called out to Gaelan. Greg and Todd—two brothers he'd known since childhood. He willed them not to come over, but of course they did. They'd be going home and telling their wives about seeing Gaelan in the bar with a pretty girl, and they'd rehash his troubled love life all over again. They might protect him from the photographers, but among themselves he was still a favourite topic of gossip.

He made the introductions and told them about the eagle. Did they know of anyone new around here? They all agreed it wouldn't be one of the locals, but then Greg said he'd heard some guy from St. John's had rented the old Crawley place and was planning to do some hunting. He said he'd check it out and get back to him. Gaelan didn't miss the wink he gave Chloe when they went to the back for Monday-night darts.

"You think that's it?" Chloe asked him after they left. "The man who rented the Crawley place?"

"We'll see," he said. "It'll be all over town soon, and if anyone knows anything, I'll hear of it."

Now that the guys were gone, he was aware of having to make conversation again. And he knew they were being watched. One eye on the dartboard and one eye on him as he drank with Sophia's pretty teacher.

* * *

ACROSS THE TABLE, Chloe was also looking rather awkward. She was tilting the glass of screech back and forth, watching the angle change with so much concentration it was as if she had made some amazing physics discovery. Her eyes were lowered, and he admired her long lashes. What was she really thinking? If all his paranoia was justified, she was sitting there scheming how to get into his bed and his money. Did he really believe that? He remembered her with the bird in her arms. That hadn't been for show. She had been genuinely concerned for the animal and Sophia.

And what was he really thinking? In the moment he'd glimpsed Chloe and seen she was safe, he'd felt something rip through his chest. And it hadn't gone away. Maybe it was love. What else could it be? It was more than the fire he had felt when he kissed her that first night. It went beyond that. At the moment he knew she was safe, he wanted to take her into his arms and keep her there forever. He drew his fingers through his thick hair, then sat for a moment, eyes closed, contemplating the enormity of the mess he had gotten himself into.

"What would you do with a billion dollars, Chloe?" It was out of his mouth before his brain could tell him to stop. And his voice contained all the edge it held when she first showed up at Widow's Cliff. It was as if he didn't believe anything good could come from love.

She looked up from the glass of screech she'd been studying with a startled look in her eyes. "Why are you asking?" she asked defensively.

Damn, he had done it again. "Just curious. You said

my scholarships . . . were generous. I guess I wondered what you would do." God, he was an idiot! What did he expect her to say? *When I have all your money, I'm going to take off with it and make your life a living hell . . .*

"You're testing me, aren't you? You still don't believe I took this job because I wanted to teach. You still think I'm after your money or something."

He was about to confess it was a test. And he opened his mouth to apologize when she shocked him by picking up the glass of screech and downing it in a single gulp. She didn't even shudder.

"You never give up, do you?" she said, leaning across the table toward him and talking in a low voice. "Let's get this straight once and for all. Would I like some of your money? Yes, I would. For starters, I would give some of it to my parents. You have no idea what it's like, do you? You've always lived at Widow's Cliff and had lots of money. I'm sure you didn't get hurt when the stock market crashed. Well, maybe you lost a few million, but what does that matter to a billionaire? For all I know, you were one of the people who profited. But it was hard on us real people. My parents lost almost all their retirement savings and had to get jobs at the Home Depot to make ends meet. They don't want to be working at their age, but they have no choice, and they're frankly lucky to have found any job in this economy. And you know what? They never complain. And at the private school where I worked, people started pulling their kids out left, right, and centre to save money, and so I lost my job, too. I was desperate and didn't want to bother my parents with my problems, so that's why I fibbed about my teaching credentials for the academy. And that's also why I took this job."

She looked as if she were giving him a chance to respond to this, but he couldn't. He was completely speechless. She looked up for a moment as if to make sure no was listening before resuming.

"Besides, how was I to know from the ad it was you? I didn't even know you existed—I never read those celebrity magazines. When Marcus said who you were, the most I could remember was reading an article some-where about philanthropist billionaires. You were listed next to Bill Gates and that guy who's always trying to fly his balloon around the world."

"Richard Branson?" He took a large swallow of Scotch.

"Right, Richard Branson." A whoop went up from the guys around the dartboard, and Chloe looked as if she'd lost her train of thought. She eyed her empty glass of screech as if she wanted more, and he thought, *Okay, that does it. I'm in love.* Determined never to fall in love again, he had done just that in less than two weeks. He looked at her and realized she was panicking a bit right now, as if wondering whether he might bite her head off, but really he just wanted to lean across the table and kiss that lovely mouth.

"Maybe we can call the vet now," she said, pulling her coat back on and looking like she just wanted to escape.

"Good idea." He'd almost forgotten about the eagle,

so intent was he on what could happen between him and this woman. Better that she had pulled away just now. He tried to imagine her reaction to all his secrets. Everything, from the beginning: Colleen, his brother, Sophia. The whole sordid story. The truth—if such a thing existed. Over the years it had become such a web of lies and deceits that he wasn't sure himself where the truth lay. How could he expect anyone to understand what he'd got himself into? He could hardly understand it himself. And while she'd been right that he really had no idea what it was like to lose one's job and work at the Home Depot, his money was of absolutely no use when it came to extricating himself from the mess he was in. Oh, he'd tried to spend his way out, but there were still some things money couldn't buy. He could list them all, starting with peace of mind.

He entered the vet's number on the cell, and a moment later was reporting back to Chloe that the bird's condition had stabilized.

Without Chloe's intervention, the vet had said, *the bird definitely would have perished.*

"Good news, then," she said, and he thought she looked a little shell-shocked. "We need to let Sophia know right away."

"You're right," he said, handing her the phone.

"You do it. You're her father. Now act like one."

She was right, of course. And if he was hoping to make a place for Chloe in his life, to convince her he wasn't some sort of monster, he knew he was going to have to start acting like a father, and a good one at that.

There was no point in explaining his web of secrets tonight. It was very possible, too, that even his best attempts wouldn't be enough to make a life with Chloe possible. Either way—telling lies or the truth—he would have to think long and hard about whether he wanted to drag someone else down into hell with him.

CHAPTER 5

CHLOE WAITED FOR HIS REACTION AND WAS surprised when he obediently took back his cell and dialled the number. She knew she'd been nervy telling him how to be a father, and now that the adrenalin from her indignant outburst was dissipating, she was expecting him to fire her yet again. But he didn't. He didn't even look angry. She thought, *If this weren't Gaelan Byrne, I'd say he looked contrite.*

He turned away from her while he spoke with Sophia, but she heard every word and couldn't at all fault him on his tone. He was honest and gentle as he explained to the child that the bird had stabilized and there was some hope that it would live, and maybe even fly again, but that there were no guarantees, and it could still take a turn for the worst. One thing was for sure, he added to Sophia, it wouldn't have stood a chance had she and Chloe not acted so quickly. He listened patiently for a moment and then concluded by saying they'd be home soon. Dropping his phone into his coat pocket, he turned to Chloe and said rather wearily, "Let's go."

She walked to the car, conscious of the locals in the bar watching them leave. She was pretty sure they were drawing some conclusions about her relationship with the "Dark Lord of the Manor," as John the bartender had called him. She was pretty sure, too, they were all comparing her to the past teachers who'd come and gone so quickly. How many had there been? The one who'd sold stories to the gossip magazines, and one or even more before that?

It also occurred to her how comfortable he'd been among these people. He trusted them, and they seemed to have enormous respect for him, and not the slightest bit of envy. It was a side of him that Windy had told her about but that she'd seen very little of herself.

He opened the car door for her and said nothing in return when she thanked him. He was silent all the way home, too. She watched him out of the corner of her eye and speculated on what he was thinking about as he watched the road ahead. Whatever it was, he was so intent, it was as if she weren't even there.

Was he going over what she'd said to him? She had really given him a piece of her mind—pretty much dared him to get angry with her—and yet he hadn't bitten at all. At the time, he'd looked surprised, and for a moment she thought she saw something else. She didn't know what, but for a strange moment she had thought he might lean across the table and kiss her—until she panicked and suggested they call the vet.

They reached the gates of Widow's Cliff. He pulled

into the drive and drove slowly through the dark tunnel of trees. When they emerged, Chloe was caught unawares by the beauty of Widow's Cliff silhouetted against the cloud-filled sky. "It's so beautiful." The words escaped unbidden, the first words that had been said since they'd stepped into the car. She said it with the awe she felt.

"That it is," Gaelan replied as he parked the car in front of what Windy called the drive shed.

He put his hand on the car door to get out. Suddenly she didn't want things to go back to the way they had been before they went into the bar. "Why don't you eat supper with us tonight?" she asked impulsively.

He let go of the handle and turned to her. She thought she'd never seen anyone look so tragic in her life. She almost wished he would get angry with her. *Anything*, she thought, *would be better than this*. "What's . . ." She was going to say *wrong* when without warning, he pulled her toward him and his mouth was on hers, his fingers grasping her hair.

It was so sudden she almost resisted, but the feeling passed in seconds as she felt like something was exploding inside her and she was kissing him back, her urgency as great as his. There was no chance she was going to pull away and slap his face this time. She didn't care where this took her or how badly it ended; she was going to go with it even if it took her over the cliff . . .

And then he was pulling away, and she was left sitting there, stunned with the image of another woman going over a cliff, her lips trembling at the intensity of this kiss.

He was out of the car now, striding around to open the passenger door for her, although she had been closer to the driver's door. He held out his hand and she took it, wondering what was to happen now, but he released her hand as soon as she was out. "I won't be having supper with you this evening," he said, and Chloe could tell he was struggling to put some normalcy in his voice. "I have to call Marcus about the meeting I missed in Montreal today."

She nodded, not trusting herself to speak.

"I'll see you tomorrow," he continued. "Maybe I can take you and Sophia out for lunch before I leave. For you and for Sophia, I will try to be a better father." They were nearing the house now, and he turned to look down at her. "I hope that kiss doesn't cause you to quit again. Because I'd really like you to stay."

She opened her mouth to say something, anything, but there was nothing she could think of to say.

"Let me go up and say good night to her, and I'll see you tomorrow." And then he cupped her face in his hands, gently now, and ran one finger over her lips. "I can tell you right now, Chloe Winters, that my greatest fear is that when you know everything there is to know, you won't want to stay another day. But will you do me a favour anyway?"

"What is it?" she asked.

"Stay here until I get back from Montreal. We can talk then. I just need to work some things out."

"Yes, of course."

He kissed her again. A sweet, brief kiss, still electrifying but also full of promise, and then he turned and left her standing there as he went into the house.

She stayed outside for a moment, deciding she would wait before going in. She would give him enough time to talk to Sophia and go to his office.

Slowly, she walked down to the cliff. She put her hands on the rail and looked out at the icebergs, listening to the waves as they crashed against the rocks.

He hadn't said his wife had died by a fall from the cliff, but now she was sure that was what had happened. Her breath caught in her chest as she remembered his kiss. She hadn't cared where it would take her or how badly it might end, she was willing to go with it even if it took her over the cliff . . . She felt suddenly cold, and it wasn't just from the ocean wind.

And him telling her that when she learned the truth, she would never stay. *He was hurt real bad*, Windy had said.

When they were in the bar, there had been a slight lifting of that cloud of anger that seemed to constantly envelop him. She sensed he wanted to trust her, to finally believe that she wasn't just trying to land herself a billionaire.

Everything went back to his wife, she was sure. *Ever since his wife . . .* A wife she was now sure had fallen from this very cliff. *And yes, my relationship with Sophia's mother was not the happiest.* How do you grieve when the person you want out of your life dies? What do you feel when the wife you no longer love falls from a cliff? Relief?

And with that relief, a terrible guilt? Is that what ate away at him? Was this what he felt would scare her away?

She walked back toward the house. Its diamond-paned windows looked down on her like eyes. He'd told her that more than one person had fallen from this cliff. The house watching as his wife slipped into oblivion. Chloe shuddered and tried to shake off these dark thoughts. She was not in a Gothic romance novel. She was a modern, intelligent woman, the teacher of the daughter of a billionaire who lived in a castle on a cliff his wife had fallen from, and whom, only minutes ago, she had been kissing and thinking . . .

"Okay, Chloe Winters," she said out loud. "Get a grip on yourself." She walked to the door of Widow's Cliff as fast as she could and resolved to spend the evening reading a book and trying not to think of Gaelan Byrne.

TRUE TO HIS word, Gaelan came by the schoolroom the next morning to take them to lunch in Puffin's Cove. "We can go and see the eagle, too. I've called the vet's, and he told me the eagle was well enough for visitors." Sophia clapped her hands and jumped up and down, which led Gaelan to add, not unkindly, "Very quiet visitors."

Chloe was surprised to see him. Although he'd told her the night before they would go for lunch, she was still surprised. Given his strange behaviour, she had expected to get up and hear he'd already left for Montreal. She had spent the evening returning a call from her parents—doing her best to sound as if her new job were going wonderfully—and then curled up with a romance novel she'd brought from home. Though she started her book wondering with every turn of the page whether he might knock on her door, much to her surprise, she actually got caught up in the story. True, while the novel's agreeable blue-eyed hero couldn't have been more different from the moody, dark-eyed Gaelan, she kept casting Gaelan in his place, and the tears she cried at the novel's end might have had something to do with her own fears that there was no room in her own story for such a satisfying conclusion.

My greatest fear is that when you know everything there is to know, you won't want to stay another day. His words kept going around her head in circles. They didn't seem to leave much room for a happy ending. Maybe if she had any sense, she should leave now. But she knew she wouldn't. She would do just what he asked. She would wait for him to return from Montreal, and she would hear what he had to say. What, short of his having murdered his wife, could make her want to leave now? As that was completely ridiculous, she assumed she was here to stay.

Once the plan to see the eagle had been made, there wasn't much Chloe could do with Sophia. The child was too excited to concentrate, and while Chloe wouldn't have called herself excited in quite the same way, she certainly was finding it hard to concentrate after seeing Gaelan again. Sophia volunteered to help Chloe pick out something different to wear into town, and Chloe decided that was as good a way as any to spend the next hour.

Gaelan was waiting for them beside the car at the allotted time, and Chloe tried to detect signs of the Gaelan who'd kissed her the night before with such fervour. In the end, she decided that while he was certainly trying to do his best to be pleasant, the same air of distraction that had settled over him on the ride home was still there, and she could only hope that on his return from Montreal there would be some answers.

He was, however, trying very hard to live up to his promise of being a better father. He even asked Sophia to choose a restaurant and didn't flinch when she shouted out McDonald's. He seemed almost . . . normal during the meal, but still, the effort worried Chloe. How many parents had to work so hard at such a simple, instinctive thing as loving their own child?

After lunch, they went to see the eagle. The vet explained it would be released when it was well enough to fly. The game warden called while they were there, saying the hunter had been caught too, thanks to Greg and Todd, the brothers she'd met at the bar. Not only had he been charged, he'd been convinced to go back to St. John's.

Sophia, overjoyed the bird was going to be okay, chattered all the way back to Widow's Cliff, and Gaelan didn't seem to mind. They parted at the classroom door, and Chloe wondered if she would see him again before he left for Montreal.

Distracted as she was, she did her best to focus on Sophia's French lesson. She could already list just about every animal she'd heard of in French. Pretty soon, they were going to be adding imaginary animals, and Chloe thought how she'd like to laugh about this with Gaelan. She decided to teach Sophia the words for *big* and *small*, so she could now have a big elephant and a small mouse, though Sophia thought it much funnier to have a big mouse and a small elephant.

At 4 p.m., she released Sophia into Windy's care. It was her first chance to be alone all day, and she decided to use the time to walk around the headland. It was cold, the temperature dropping with the sun, and a bitter wind blew in from the sea.

Wearing Windy's coat again, she headed toward the cliff, stopping in her tracks when she saw Gaelan there, all dark and handsome, silhouetted against the sky. "Okay if I join you?" she asked.

"Of course. You look cold. And that coat of Windy's makes you look like some old fisherman's wife."

"My own coat was ruined when we saved the bird."

"Right. I forgot. I'll have one sent for you from St. John's tomorrow. The calendar might say spring, but around here we could see winter weather into June."

"Thank you," she said. "That's very generous of you. And it is cold."

"There's snow tonight in the forecast." He took his cashmere scarf and wrapped it around her neck, his fingers brushing her skin as he tied it. The scarf carried his scent of soap and ocean winds, and he was so close she wondered if he was going to kiss her again. But instead he turned his gaze back to the ocean.

"Thank you for taking Sophia and me to see the eagle today," she said. "It made her very happy. Did you know she wants to be an ornithologist when she grows up?"

"Really? And she really said that? 'Ornithologist'?"

"Yes. It was pretty cute." She could have sworn there was a note of pride in his voice.

"I guess she gets her environmentalism streak from you," she ventured further.

His face darkened, and Chloe braced herself for his anger. Just when she'd thought they were doing okay. "I'm not so sure about that," was all he said, rather sadly.

"What do you mean?"

He just looked at her. "Let's just leave this where we left it last night, okay? When I get back, I promise." He pointed out over the water. "Do you see that plume of water?"

"A whale, right?" Any other time she would have been interested.

"It's a humpback. I've never seen one this early in the season. They come up from the Caribbean. Maybe it'll be an early spring after all." The enormous animal's tail lifted high in the air before disappearing entirely beneath the waves. "They're beautiful animals. They were almost hunted to extinction a few decades back, and while they still get caught in fishing lines, they are making a comeback." Chloe had the feeling he was talking about the animal to avoid personal conversation. But then, at least he was talking. "Maybe we can take Sophia whale watching next month. She's probably old enough now."

"I'm sure she'd love it. Look, there it goes again." Chloe was only a few feet from the rail fence, but she went closer as if the few extra feet might provide her with a better view.

Gaelan roughly grabbed her arm and pulled her back. "Don't get too close!" he said sharply.

"There's a fence," she protested. "I was perfectly safe." He had spoken sharply to her—but it wasn't anger, it was fear. She hastened to reassure him. "It's okay," she said quietly. "I'm absolutely fine." And then she knew she wouldn't wait for him to return from Montreal. She suddenly just needed to know. "Is that what happened to . . . ?" She couldn't quite get up the nerve to add *your wife*.

He ignored her completely. "I'm driving out to St. John's tonight. I'll be staying there overnight and leaving for my office in Montreal first thing in the morning. Like I said last night, I'll be back in just over a week. And, please—stay back from the cliff."

FRIDAY MORNING FOUND Windy at the schoolroom door. "Chloe, my nephew Cullen's got something for you by the drive shed."

Sophia tore after Windy as she left the room, and Chloe could do nothing but follow her down the stairs and out the front door. On the drive was a brand-new white Jeep.

"It's from Mr. Byrne," Cullen explained as he handed her the keys and registration. "He called from St. John's before leaving for Montreal and asked me to arrange it all."

She gaped at the registration, speechless. The car was in her name. It was hers—a gift from Gaelan. An extremely generous gift. *Well, I guess the job really is mine now*, she thought. *I'm going to be staying here for a while after all.* She refused to contemplate whether it meant more than just having a job.

After Cullen left, she'd called Gaelan's cellphone to thank him, but it was off and she felt awkward leaving a message. She'd try again later. Just as she put down the phone, the doorbell rang again. It was a courier with a parcel from St. John's. Inside was a beautiful new coat, along with a note.

Chloe—Here is the promised coat. When a man buys a woman a coat, it's usually made of fur, but as you might have guessed, I'm not all that keen on fur. I figured you probably weren't either. I hope it's the right size and that you like it. —Gaelan

Like it? She loved it. It was long and warm and a beautiful shade of forest green.

She wore it for the drive to Puffin's Cove, and after dropping Sophia off at her class, she parked her new Jeep on the main street and walked down to the harbour, which was still choked with ice. The boats lined up on the shore were still shrouded in their winter wrappers. A raucous group of gulls fought over the remains of a dead fish, their cries filling the cold air. Most of the town's cafés and shops were closed until the summer tourist season, but Chloe found a bookshop, where she purchased a book on the history of Newfoundland. She tried calling Gaelan again to thank him for the gifts, but again only got his voicemail. She'd try again later.

She walked around the harbour, admiring the stark beauty of the weather-beaten, greyed shops and houses. It was nice to have this afternoon to herself, especially knowing that Sophia was getting some much-needed time with children her own age. But Chloe was also aware of a melancholy loneliness. She told herself it was natural. She was far from her family, she had no friends here—and, it seemed, no longer in Boston either, thanks to Shawn—and she was living in an isolated place.

But she knew it was more than that. It was Gaelan, his dark eyes and deep voice finding their way into her dreams day and night. The sound of a footstep either imagined or real would make her heart beat louder. What did he mean to tell her when he returned? Because it seemed now that he did want to trust her and believe her. Those kisses a few nights ago had pretty much been proof he wanted something more than just an employer-employee relationship. And not just sex. Something more. A lot more. She would be happy but for his warning. Yesterday she had convinced herself it was the relief he felt over his wife's accidental death. If, of course, that was really what had happened. But what else could it be? What could make her want to leave now?

The wind off the harbour was icy, and the sky was leaden in colour. By the end of the day, snow or rain would start to fall. Chloe hoped it would hold off until they were home. She hated the thought of driving along the coast road in bad weather. Despite her gloves, Chloe's hands were cold, and she slipped them into the pockets of her new coat. She turned around and headed back toward the row of shops near the entrance to the harbour. On her way in, she had seen a restaurant with an "open" sign in the window. She would have a cup of coffee and read her new book until it was time to pick up Sophia.

The restaurant was bright and cheerful with checked tablecloths and matching café curtains in the windows. A couple with a child about Sophia's age sat at one of the tables. They seemed happy and comfortable together, and she thought back to her trip to McDonald's with Gaelan and Sophia. Had people looked at them and thought the same?

She walked to the back of the restaurant to take a table as far from the door as possible. She was just taking off her coat when she saw him. Gaelan. He was sitting at the bar reading a newspaper, a bottle of beer at his elbow. She stopped in her tracks, and it seemed that her heart stopped, too. What was he doing here? He was supposed to be in Montreal!

She had taken a hesitant step in his direction when he looked up from his newspaper and turned his head toward her and smiled. She took a faltering step back.

"I . . . I'm sorry," she stammered. The man on the stool was not Gaelan!

She didn't know how she could even tell, the resemblance was so remarkable. The same thick dark hair, eyes, build, and features, but something was fundamentally different, something that gave him away immediately, although for a moment she didn't know what it was. "I thought you were someone else," she said, but without conviction. Really, it was amazing. He smiled again at her, and now she knew what the difference was. The smile! Gaelan would never smile this easily. It would seem frivolous of him. Besides, his intensity would never allow it. He was like the hero in a Gothic novel who carried in his very being the dark and stormy night.

"Can I guess who you thought I was?" he asked, still smiling at her, his eyes full of curiosity. His voice, too, was different. Lighter, friendlier, but lacking the richness that made Gaelan's so sexy. She nodded, knowing by his lack of surprise that this had happened before.

"I'm Bowen Byrne, Gaelan Byrne's twin brother," he said as he held his hand out to her. She took it, and his grip was warm and firm.

"I'm Chloe Winters," she said. "I didn't know Gaelan had a twin."

"Alas," he said with an exaggerated Newfoundland accent, "not many people do. My brother and I are not exactly on speaking terms. And you? How do you know my brother?"

Chloe hesitated, absorbing what he had said about

not being on speaking terms. "I work for him. I'm Sophia's tutor," she said.

Again that smile. "How is Sophia? I haven't seen her since her mother died. She was such a bright little thing."

"She still is," Chloe said, hearing the pride in her own voice. Suddenly, she wondered what Bowen could tell her. *It's not just curiosity*, she told herself. Although there was lots of that—but it was more important she knew something about Sophia's mother so as to better understand the situation and help Sophia. Surely the loss of her mother meant something to her, and Gaelan's refusal to discuss her could only be unhealthy. And Windy was as close-mouthed as Gaelan when it came to the topic. "May I sit down?" she asked.

"Yes, of course. I'm sorry. You must think I'm terribly rude."

Chloe smiled. "Not at all," she said, taking the stool beside him. Compared to his brother Gaelan, Bowen was extremely polite. Bowen was every bit as good-looking as Gaelan, although a little fairer—she saw that now as the other difference in their looks—but at the same time, charming and relaxed. She liked him already.

"May I buy you a drink?" he asked, folding up the newspaper and laying it aside.

"Just coffee," she said. "I have to pick up Sophia from her enrichment class at three."

"Fine, coffee it is," he said, signalling the waiter. "How long have you been at Widow's Cliff?"

"Just over two weeks."

He nodded, and Chloe sensed he was as curious about her as she was about him. "Not long," he said wryly. "But still probably a record. You and my brother must be getting along famously."

She smiled nervously, surprised at the sudden prick of tears at the corners of her eyes. It was as if in that moment all the stress and confusing emotions were catching up to her.

Bowen placed his hand over hers and gave it a slight squeeze before taking it away again. It was a familiar gesture, and Chloe felt like they could be friends—that he understood a little of what she was going through. "It's okay," he said soothingly. "You don't have to explain. I know my brother probably better than anyone."

Chloe took a sip of coffee and breathed deeply in order to regain her composure. She wondered if she were acting inappropriately. If the brothers weren't on speaking terms, should she be speaking with Bowen? This wasn't a situation she had any experience with. But maybe there was something here that could help her understand him better. Besides, the mystery was driving her crazy. Hadn't she just proved that when she almost started crying? "Why aren't you on speaking terms?" she asked.

"Sophia's mother," he said quietly. "Colleen."

Chloe knew this was getting very personal, but she plunged on. "Gaelan doesn't let Sophia talk about her mother. Do you know why?"

Bowen shrugged. "Guilt, maybe. If Gaelan is capable

of such a thing." He took a sip of his beer. "How much do you want to know?"

Any warning bells still ringing in Chloe's head about being indiscreet were now entirely drowned out by her overwhelming curiosity to find out the truth about Gaelan. The only computer she'd seen in the castle had been in Gaelan's office, and she worried too much about Gaelan finding out she'd been snooping on the Internet. In Boston, she hadn't had enough money to keep up the payments on her smartphone and hadn't yet had a chance to get a new one here. But then, everything about his personal life on the Internet was likely to be gossip, anyway. So Bowen was her only opportunity to really learn about Gaelan. *Everything. Tell me everything*, she thought to herself, while out loud she said, "Tell me about Sophia's mother."

The waitress asked Bowen if he would like another beer. He declined and ordered a coffee instead. "Like you, I'm driving—which reminds me. I parked my car just up the hill, and I should put some money in the parking meter." He stood up. "Is your car okay? These meters only have an hour on them."

"I should probably do the same. I'll come with you."

"No, wait here where it's warm."

"Thanks," she said. "It's the white Jeep in front of the drugstore."

She held a dollar coin out to him, but he waved it away. "No problem, just don't let anyone take my stool."

Chloe ordered another coffee for herself, and Bowen

got back just as it arrived. He sat down a little breathlessly. "You wanted to know about Colleen."

Chloe nodded, hoping she didn't look as eager as she felt.

Bowen stirred his coffee slowly as if deciding where to begin. "It's hard to know where to start. Colleen was my girlfriend first. I met her in New York. A friend of mine was in a play off Broadway, and I went to see him in it. And there she was." His voice was full of sadness. "I thought she was the most gorgeous woman I'd ever seen. My friend introduced us, and I'd like to think it was love."

Chloe could see that it upset him to talk about this. "If this is too hard for you . . ." Chloe began reluctantly.

"No," he said firmly. "It was a long time ago. It's good therapy for me. And you're a good listener." He sipped his coffee. "Everything was fine until I introduced her to the family. Gaelan seemed jealous. He's the older twin, which is why he has Widow's Cliff. Ours is an old-fashioned family, everything to the oldest child, and I guess Gaelan figured that also meant my girlfriend. Anyway, Gaelan managed to win her away from me. He poured on the charm, and with all his money, he could promise her the world. And I'm afraid she fell for it.

"But after she married him, she discovered what he was really like—cold and jealous. And the isolation of Widow's Cliff really got to her. She was a model and an actress from New York City, and she went near crazy wandering around that creepy castle all by herself. She already felt she was a prisoner there, and then she had Sophia."

He paused and ran his fingers through his hair. It was a gesture she had seen Gaelan make, and she was struck again by their similarities—at least in looks and gestures. When it came to personalities, they were miles apart.

"Windy said Colleen didn't love Sophia," Chloe said. "Is that true?"

Bowen looked at her with a puzzled expression on his face. "Windy's a good soul but pretty traditional, and I think she's the only person in the world who believes that Gaelan can do no wrong. I don't think she approved of Colleen wanting another life beyond that of mother and lady of the manor."

"So Colleen didn't keep up her career?"

"How could she? Every time she tried to get to New York for an audition, he'd have an excuse that kept her from going. The weather was too bad to go to the airport . . . He had something more important . . . You name it, he came up with it. I think he liked to keep her where he could keep an eye on her."

"Why?"

"Because she was miserable, and he didn't want her to get away from him. She was like everything else is to him—a possession," he said bitterly. "To make a long story short, she emailed me. She was terribly depressed. We arranged to meet in St. John's the next week. I was going to ask her to come back with me to New York, but she never arrived."

Chloe felt a cold chill. "What happened?"

"She went for a walk along the cliff and never came back." He swallowed hard. "Her body was never found. The official explanation was that she fell from the cliff and the tide carried out her body."

"But the fence . . ."

"I said that was the official explanation. There are gates along the fence. They think she used one of the gates to get closer to the edge and then . . ."

Chloe paused to let Bowen recover his voice. "You don't sound convinced," she said softly. "Do you think she committed suicide?"

"Colleen was deathly afraid of heights. She was incapable of going anywhere near the edge of that cliff."

Chloe absorbed the full meaning of what he was trying to tell her. "You don't think Gaelan . . . ?" Chloe asked in horror. She remembered looking out over the ocean and wondering, what, short of his having murdered his wife, could make her want to leave now. She had dismissed it as ridiculous, and yet . . .

Bowen shrugged. "Forget it," he said resignedly. "Maybe it was just an accident," he added without conviction. "I just think my brother was a little too quick to agree with the accident verdict. He even denied that she was afraid of heights."

Chloe didn't know what to say. Bowen seemed reluctant to accuse his brother, but she could tell the doubts were there, eating away at him. Just as they were at her.

He suddenly straightened and smiled at her. "Don't

listen to me. I'm just a man who had his heart broken. Now let's talk about something else—I feel bad that our first meeting had to be so heavy."

Chloe agreed. "But I don't know that it could have been any different. Given the circumstances."

"I suppose so," he said. "Do you think I could see you again? I promise to be fun and entertaining."

Chloe thought for a moment. "I don't know. What would Gaelan say?"

Bowen laughed bitterly. "Gaelan doesn't have to know. Don't forget you only work for him."

Chloe felt suddenly defiant. After all Bowen had told her, she didn't think she owed Gaelan much loyalty at all. "How's Sunday?" Gaelan would still be away.

"Of course. Shall we meet here? I bet you haven't seen many of the sights since you've arrived."

Chloe shook her head, and they arranged a time to meet. Bowen insisted on paying the bill, and she let him. With her thoughts in turmoil, she walked back to the Jeep. No wonder Gaelan had said she would leave the moment he told her. It had been the only thing she could think of that would make her leave, and now here was Bowen telling her just that. Did she now wait for Gaelan to get back and tell her in his own words? While Bowen had no proof that Gaelan was involved in his wife's death, what he'd revealed to her was damning enough.

But then she remembered Sophia. Surely she couldn't leave her with such a man. *No*, she told herself firmly, *it's my responsibility now to look after Sophia.*

And who was to say this wasn't just speculation on Bowen's part, too? He'd loved Colleen, the brothers had had a falling out, and he was ready to believe the worst of Gaelan. What if it was just what she'd thought it was all along? Gaelan's marriage to Colleen was an unhappy one. She'd fallen from the cliff, and he felt guilty because he'd been relieved. But what about Bowen's tales of possessiveness and jealousy? Did that fit with the Gaelan she knew? Had this anger that she'd convinced herself was the result of his unhappy marriage been there all along? Should she be sympathizing with Colleen, as Bowen said? If she didn't leave now, would she find herself at the mercy of a jealous man? More than once she had thought that with a woman's love, he might change, might start to feel something for Sophia, for herself. Really, she had been behaving like a lovesick schoolgirl.

She climbed into the Jeep and put the key in the ignition but didn't turn it yet. *No*, she thought. *This is not a Gothic romance. Get a grip.* Gaelan didn't kill his wife. Bowen was only speculating, and who was to say he didn't want revenge on his brother by turning Chloe against him? And she couldn't expect him to be a fair judge of Gaelan's treatment of Colleen—he was jealous. No. She would wait until Gaelan came back from Montreal. She would hear what he had to say, and she would go from there.

She took a deep breath and turned the key. It made a few grinding noises, then nothing. She swore under her breath and leaned her head against the steering wheel.

Now what? Sophia's class would be over in fifteen minutes. How would they get home? Knowing it was useless, she turned the key again. The result was the same. How could this happen to a brand-new vehicle?

Suddenly there was a sharp knock on the window. Startled, she looked up. It was Bowen.

"Problems?" he said.

Chloe rolled down the window. "It won't start."

"Oh, no! It's going to be tough to find someone to fix it on a Friday afternoon."

"Great," she said in exasperation. "I've got to pick up Sophia."

"Come on, I'll drive you home. You can call a garage tomorrow."

She thought for a moment. Maybe Windy's nephew could take care of it. She could ask Windy to call him later. "Okay, thanks a lot," she said, getting out and grabbing Sophia's booster seat from the back of the Jeep.

It wasn't until they were parked in front of the church where Sophia's class was being held that Chloe suddenly saw the flaw in her plan. "Sophia," she said suddenly. "Isn't she going to recognize you?"

"I doubt it. I haven't seen her in four years."

"But you look like her father."

He shrugged. "Don't worry. They say everyone has a twin somewhere. Just go get her—everything will be fine."

And it was. Sophia did a slight double take at seeing Bowen, but on deciding that he wasn't her father, didn't remark on the likeness. She had more important things to talk about. One of the students had brought in his puppy, and Chloe was regaled with a moment-by-moment description of the puppy's antics.

They drove along the coast. On their left was a rock cut, and signs warned of falling rocks. On the right, a guardrail marked the edge of the shoulder and the beginning of a rocky descent to the ocean. They were about five miles out of town when the clouds finally let go and the rain came down in a sudden torrent. Bowen cursed and slowed the car down to a crawl. "It's freezing on the road," he said, straining to see through the downpour. "I just suddenly remembered why I hate this bloody province—winter ten months of the year."

Taken aback by his language, Chloe suggested they find a spot to pull over until the worst of the rain had passed. She looked behind her to check on Sophia and was horrified to see that the girl had taken off her seatbelt and was leaning over the back of her seat. "Sophia!" Chloe said sharply. "Put your seatbelt back on! Bowen, please pull over, so I can do up Sophia's seatbelt!"

"I can't," Bowen said through clenched teeth. "Not here."

"I want to show you my picture of the puppy," Sophia said. "It's in my backpack."

"You can show me when you get home. Please sit down. Bowen . . ."

Just then Bowen cursed again, and Chloe wheeled around to see a truck coming toward them, swerving from side to side as the driver struggled to keep it on the road. Everything else happened in a blur. Bowen slammed on the brakes and turned the wheel hard to the left, and Chloe saw the truck, the rock cut, the ocean, and the sky whirling around them as if their car were a spinning top. Sophia screamed in the back of the car, and Chloe turned in her seat. Straining against the momentum of the spinning car, she reached for Sophia, praying the child would not be thrown through the windshield, and waited for the crash.

"MON DIEU, GAELAN!" Marcus said in exasperation from behind his desk. "You are going to wear out the carpet with that infernal pacing. Not only that, you haven't heard a single word I've said to you. Now sit down and tell me what is going on."

Gaelan didn't answer but instead went to the window and looked out over the city of Montreal. Marcus's office was on the fortieth floor of the glass and steel building that housed Byrne Enterprises. The floor-to-ceiling windows afforded an excellent view. The building marked the edge of the modern city, and below them, the old city, with its labyrinth of cobbled streets and stone buildings, stretched between them and the harbour, which was still peppered with the remains of the winter's ice. Gaelan liked this view, liked to think of the river flowing out of the city toward the ocean and his home on Widow's Cliff. It was a grey day, but as yet there had been no rain.

"Come on," Marcus urged. "Tell me what's going on. You've been here since Wednesday, shutting yourself up in your office, but as far as I can tell, you haven't done a single thing—or at least anything related to Byrne Enterprises."

Gaelan turned and looked at Marcus as if to say, *Just who's the boss here, anyway?*

In his bespoke Savile Row suit, Marcus actually looked more the part of the boss. Gaelan, on the other hand, hated suits and instead wore a creamy wool shirt and jeans. He refused to wear a tie on any occasion, and his business acquaintances knew it was useless to print *black tie* on his invitations—he would dress as he pleased. It killed them, too, that Gaelan could carry off a shirt and jeans with the elegance of a tuxedo and turn the head of every woman in the room.

"You've also been avoiding me," Marcus said. "You haven't even told me how you made out with Sophia's new tutor."

"How I made out?" Gaelan hooked his thumbs into the belt loops of his jeans and leaned a shoulder against the glass. "Then I guess I was right in thinking you were more interested in finding me a girlfriend than Sophia a teacher."

Marcus grinned. "Well, how did *I* make out then?"

Gaelan turned his attention to the view. His eyes were full of dark emotion. "I should probably fire you. You didn't even check her references. But perhaps I should thank you instead."

"Then you like her?" Marcus asked, sounding pleased with himself.

"Who wouldn't?" Gaelan said. "She's gorgeous, sexy, smart, and already she adores Sophia. But I can't drag her into the mess I've made of my life."

"Come on. Doesn't love always find a way?"

"Maybe in songs and movies, Marcus."

"Just level with her. Tell her the whole story. Colleen, Sophia, Bowen."

"You're right, and I plan to do just that when I get back. But I'm not sure even I know the whole story, Marcus."

"Look, after all this time I think you can conclude you do. Forget the crazy theories. All those private detectives you've hired have turned up nothing. Get on with your life. Make a fresh start with Chloe. You deserve it."

Gaelan shrugged. Marcus made it sound so easy.

"So, where is that brother of yours now, anyway?" Marcus asked.

"I don't know. He's not in Greece anymore. The number I had for him is out of service." Gaelan had also tried calling a number in Italy, but there had been no answer. Marcus was right—he should just get on with his life. After all this time, his theories *were* starting to sound a little crazy.

He suppressed a sigh and returned to the problem of Bowen. "Bowen was probably chased out the country by some irate husband. But he'll show up—he always does, whenever the money runs out. And I have this bad feeling he's overdue for a visit."

"I don't know how you put up with the guy. Surely, he could be wealthy in his own right by now."

"He has been, several times over. I know it, I wrote the cheques. But money runs through his fingers like water. I guess being an international playboy is expensive."

"Sounds like a lot more fun than working, too." Marcus got up from behind his desk and went to the drinks cabinet. "Scotch? It's Friday afternoon. I think we can call it quits. If that's okay with you, boss."

"I think we can allow that," Gaelan said with one of his rare laughs. He went and sat on the leather couch, putting his feet up on the coffee table. It was a relief to talk about it. Marcus brought back the drinks and took an armchair across from Gaelan. "I think Bowen still thinks he's on the stage. But now he writes his own dramas with himself as the poor misunderstood hero at the centre."

"He's good at it, too," Marcus said. "I've always wondered if Colleen might have been his victim rather than anything else."

"Well, you can stop wondering. She had just as big a part to play as he did. Colleen was no victim. Two of a kind, that pair. Now, every time I meet a woman, I wonder if Bowen is waiting in the wings, setting me up, like he did with Colleen."

"Have you told Chloe about Sophia?" Marcus asked.

Gaelan shook his head. "No. But she made it pretty

plain to me on the first day that she thought I was a terrible father."

Marcus laughed. "And so you are."

Gaelan laughed too, but hollowly. *Thank God for Scotch*, he thought just as his cell rang. He took it from his pocket and put it to his ear without checking the display. "Gaelan Byrne," he said.

There was a rush of words at the other end. It was impossible for Gaelan to make them out, although he did recognize Windy's voice.

"Slow down, Windy! I can't understand a word."

"Oh Gaelan, it's Sophia! There's been an accident, a car accident on Cliff Road! She was with Chloe. Oh, Gaelan, I'm so worried! Chloe phoned me from the hospital. Sophia's unconscious, and they don't know how bad it is."

Gaelan felt himself go cold. "Where is she?"

"The children's hospital in St. John's. Chloe's with her."

"Chloe's all right?"

"Yes, but she's pretty upset."

"I'll fly there right now. You get your sister to stay with you, okay?"

There was a pause, and Gaelan pictured Windy nodding into the receiver rather than answering.

"Try not to worry," he said, knowing such words were useless. After telling her he would call her from the hospital, he shoved the phone back into his pocket.

"Come on, Marcus. You have to drive me to the airport. I have to fly back to St. John's immediately. I'll call my pilot on the way to alert her."

Marcus was already on his feet, grabbing his coat from the hook beside the door. Gaelan put on his own long black coat, and the two of them were down the elevator and to the car in minutes. "What happened, Gaelan?" Marcus asked as they almost ran.

"It's Sophia," Gaelan explained. "There's been a car accident. I don't know how bad it is, but Windy says Sophia is unconscious." Gaelan was amazed by his own fear for the child. This was the second time in a week he'd been scared into recognizing his feelings for someone. Only Chloe hadn't been hurt, and Sophia was. Maybe seriously. Maybe even fatally.

The moment he boarded his jet, he dropped down into his seat, impatient for takeoff. He had taken only his cell with him, but not his briefcase, let alone a laptop, and he sat with his hands shoved deep into the pockets of his long black coat, willing them not to shake.

The flight was a bad one as the plane rocked with turbulence, but Gaelan was oblivious to it. He stared out the window without even registering the threat as the pilot brought the plane up through the black clouds. All he could think of was Sophia. He thought of the times she had wanted his attention and how he had walked away from her, refusing to be the father she needed. And she had no mother—not that Colleen had been much of a mother, but he certainly wouldn't win any awards as a father. Not since Colleen had told him . . . He uttered a prayer that he might have a second chance.

The pilot announced the landing. It was two degrees

Celsius in St. John's and raining. The flight had taken less than two hours, but it had seemed forever to Gaelan. He ran out though the gate, grabbed the first cab outside the terminal, and ordered the driver to take him to the hospital.

CHLOE WAS SITTING next to the bed holding Sophia's hand when Gaelan stormed breathlessly into the room.

Chloe jumped from her chair, anxious to relieve the look of fear on his face. "She's going to be okay," she said in an urgent whisper. "She's just sleeping now."

"Thank God!" he said with relief. He leaned over the sleeping girl and kissed her gently on the forehead, water dripping from his coat and hair onto the white sheets and the girl's equally white face.

She stirred without opening her eyes. "Daddy?" she whispered.

"Yes, it's me, Sophia. Everything is going to be okay."

She nodded. "I'm going to go to sleep now, okay?"

"Yes, I'll see you in the morning, honey."

Chloe watched as he stroked Sophia's hair for a moment, wondering how she could ever have thought that Gaelan Byrne did not love his daughter. It was just a shame it took a near tragedy to make him show it.

The doctor came into the room, and he and Gaelan spoke quietly next to Sophia's bed. Everything was going to be okay. Only a mild concussion. Sophia had been lucky.

Suddenly Chloe felt a wave of exhaustion wash over her. For a moment she wondered if she were going to faint, and she leaned back against the door for support. The last few hours had been horrific, and she could hardly remember the details of the crash. The sound of squealing tires as the car swung around and the crunch of metal as it crashed into the guardrail. The much louder crash of the truck as it hit the rock cut head on. Somewhere in this hospital was the truck driver, miraculously alive with only minor injuries.

Chloe recalled the fear as she had waited for the ambulance, Sophia unconscious in her arms. And where was Bowen? She remembered him talking to the police, recalled him there when the ambulance arrived, but then he was gone. She supposed he didn't want to stick around and face his brother, but she couldn't help thinking he had been cowardly, leaving her alone with Sophia.

She wondered what she should tell Gaelan. She could imagine his fury when he found out she had been with his brother. Not that the accident was Bowen's fault, but she had a feeling he'd be angry with her for having accepted the ride with him.

As she stood watching Gaelan and Sophia, she tried to remember the things Bowen had said about Gaelan: Gaelan had stolen his girlfriend and may have played a role in his own wife's death. Somehow now they sounded like sour grapes, the paranoia of a jealous brother. There had been an investigation, after all, and Colleen's death had been ruled an accident. Chloe felt ashamed for taking Bowen's side against Gaelan and wondered how she was going to tell Gaelan she had been with his brother—not to mention that his brother had been driving when the accident occurred.

Gaelan turned and looked at her, his eyes still full of tenderness. "You okay?" he asked gently.

She nodded but tears welled up in her eyes all the same. "I'm so sorry," she murmured without elaborating all her reasons for being so.

He took her in his arms, and she rested her head against the softness of his shirt. His heart beat strongly against her cheek. "There's nothing to be sorry for," he murmured. "I'm just glad you're both safe." There was a catch in his voice.

She stood there in the circle of his arms trying to grasp all that was happening. She was safe, Sophia was safe, and Gaelan had shown her how much he loved his daughter. She had been wrong to talk to Bowen—it was absurd to think Gaelan could have had something to do with his wife's death.

Just then, the nurse came in and told them it was time to leave. "We can't stay with her tonight?" Gaelan asked.

The nurse shook her head. "New rules. But don't worry. She's completely fine. We just want her to get a good night's sleep. Go get some sleep yourself."

Gaelan thanked her and, after extracting a promise that she would give him a call if Sophia should so much as stir, he picked up Chloe's coat. "We'll come back first thing in the morning. You look like you need more rest than a hard chair tonight anyway."

Chloe nodded and let him help her into her coat.

The nearby hotel was undergoing renovations in preparation for the tourist season, and with the exception of the honeymoon suite, the available rooms were booked. Gaelan took the suite, and they both laughed a little self-consciously at the heart-shaped hot tub and heart-shaped bed. But the gas fireplace and view, they agreed, were very nice. The hotel was one of the tallest buildings in St. John's, and below them, the lights of the city sparkled. Beyond lay the dark expanse of the ocean.

Wordlessly, Gaelan helped her out of her coat and hung it in the armoire beside his own.

Chloe stood where he left her, feeling awkward in this room that was so obviously for making love.

"Thank you for the coat," she said. "And the car too. They're wonderful, but it's too much."

"I wanted to," he said warmly. "And you're very welcome. Champagne?" he asked, pulling a bottle from the bar fridge. "We may not be on our honeymoon, but we can toast the fact that you and Sophia are safe."

Chloe nodded her approval as the cork popped out of the bottle. Perhaps a drink would make her feel less awkward. She wished she could think of some conversation, but other than confessing her meeting with Bowen, she could not. And she didn't want to explain that. Not now. She would explain later, and she would make him understand.

But then, suddenly, she knew she had to confess. If anything should happen between them tonight—and she was fairly sure it would—she couldn't let this stand between them. She wanted the air to be free so she could give herself wholly and completely, no secrets. She knew Gaelan had wanted to tell her his secrets as soon as he returned home, but after the accident, her secret seemed much more pressing.

"Gaelan, there's something I should tell you about the accident," she said, taking a glass.

"Not now," he said softly. "You and Sophia are safe. That's all that matters to me. I can rest easy now."

He clinked his glass against hers, and Chloe sipped her champagne, conscious of his dark eyes on hers and the closeness of his body. It was going to be okay. It was going to be wonderful. She'd tell him later, and he would understand . . .

"I think I'll take a shower," she said. She was aware of the dirt on her clothes from the accident, and she wanted to feel clean again, to wash away the scent of Bowen's car and the smell of the hospital.

Gaelan had a mischievous glint in his dark eyes. "Are you sure you don't want to try out the hot tub?" he asked slyly.

She blushed, and as fast as it had appeared, the mischievous glint was gone from his eyes and he was looking at her with a hungry intensity. He touched her face, his strong fingers tracing the outline of her lips like a kiss, and she trembled under his touch.

"Take your shower then," he said in a low voice. "I'll be here." He moved away and went to the window. Chloe went to the bathroom and stripped off her clothes with shaking hands. She stood under the hot needles of water and felt purified, ready, and very suddenly nearly crazy with desire.

She stepped from the shower and without drying the water from her body, wrapped herself in the white silk bathrobe that hung on the back of the door.

He was standing by the fireplace when she came out of the bathroom and walked toward him on trembling legs. "God, you're beautiful," he murmured as he looked at her with those dark eyes.

She remembered how rough and greedy his kisses had been that very first night they'd met. But this was different. His mouth savoured hers in deep warm kisses that said *we have all night* . . .

His hands explored the planes of her face and the curve of her throat. Tracing the neckline of the silk robe with enticing slowness, his fingers found the rise of her breast before moving to follow the line of her spine, the curve of her back . . .

"I want to make love to you," he murmured into her ear. "Is that okay?"

"Yes," she breathed against his chest.

"You won't slap me across the face then?" he whispered teasingly.

In response, Chloe put her arms around his neck and, burying her fingers in his thick hair, brought his mouth back to her own, her kisses demanding fulfilment.

He pulled her against himself, and she felt his hardness against her. He moaned, a soft sound of desire breathed against her lips.

She found the buttons on his shirt and unfastened them, wanting this barrier removed from between them. Her hands found his warm skin and the hard muscles of his abdomen. She had never felt like this with Shawn or any of her other so-called lovers. She had never felt this level of need or hunger for another man's body, nor had another man ever desired her so much. She could feel it in his touch. There was an urgency in his body, but there was also restraint, and Chloe knew that before the night was over she would go to heaven and back.

His mouth still on hers, Gaelan lifted Chloe in his arms and carried her to the ludicrous heart-shaped bed. Tearing back the satin cover, he laid her on the cool satin sheets, seating himself on the edge of the bed. He broke off the kiss and untied her robe, opening it slowly, his breathing heavy with expectation. "You are so beautiful," he repeated. His voice, barely a whisper, was full of awe and delight, and Chloe had never felt so beautiful in her life. He touched her reverently, his hands and eyes exploring her body with amazement.

He stopped and removed his shirt, and she lifted a hand from the sheets to touch the hard muscles of his chest, longing to feel his weight on hers. Her body arched toward his in anticipation.

She cringed when the phone in the pocket of his shirt, now lying on the floor, rang, intruding on their love-making with its insistent demand to be paid attention to. Gaelan looked at it as if he might throw it through the window, then he swore.

"Damn, it's Windy. I forgot to phone her and tell her Sophia was doing better. The poor woman has probably been sitting by the phone worrying herself sick." He dug the phone out of the pocket and kissed Chloe on the lips. "I'm sorry. Remind me after where I was." He glanced at the phone display, confirming it was Windy before lifting it to his cheek.

"Windy, I'm so sorry," he said. "She's fine. She's going to be all right."

There was a pause. Chloe could not hear Windy's voice. "Yes," Gaelan said, "I'm with Chloe. We're staying in St. John's for the night. We're going back to the hospital first thing in the morning." Gaelan looked into Chloe's face and smiled, and Chloe knew she could not bear a life that wasn't rewarded with Gaelan's smile.

But suddenly the smile was gone. Gaelan rose sharply from the edge of the bed and, turning his back to Chloe, strode to the window. He raised his fist, and for a moment Chloe thought he might put it through the window. He did bring it against the window but in a controlled anger that knew its strength, his fist landing noiselessly against the glass. Chloe felt frightened and twisted her body into a sitting position, unconsciously pulling up the covers to conceal her nakedness.

Gaelan wheeled around to face her, his eyes full of anger and disgust. He threw his cell into an armchair, and Chloe wondered for a moment if Gaelan was capable of physical violence after all.

"Bowen!" He nearly spat the word at her. "Does that name mean anything to you?"

CHAPTER 6

CHLOE LOOKED AT GAELAN, AND HER HEART fell. "I—" she stammered, wondering how she could prove her innocence and knowing that it was useless. His eyes, which had been so tender only moments before, were now hard and cold.

"Oh, don't bother. Windy said the police reported Bowen as driving the car." He strode over to the bed. Afraid, Chloe scrambled to the other side, still holding the covers over her body.

He leaned over and scooped up his shirt from the carpet. He straightened and put it on, his eyes never leaving Chloe. "I guess I should congratulate you. You're very good. Not only did you have me convinced, you fooled Marcus too. When I think of how many things could have gone wrong with your plan up until now—well, it's pretty remarkable you got this far." He did the buttons of his shirt and tucked it in, then picked up his cell from the chair and dropped it in his pocket. "So who are you really, Chloe Winters? One of Bowen's acting friends?"

With the blankets pulled up over her nakedness, Chloe felt exposed, vulnerable, and very, very confused. "I don't know what you're talking about," she protested. "I never even heard of Bowen until today."

"Look, Chloe, the game's over—give it up. I just can't believe I fell for the same scheme twice. First Colleen and now you. What was the plan? Marry me and then divorce me for half? Live happily ever after with my brother? Or was it strictly a business deal, with you two splitting the proceeds?" He ran his fingers through his hair. "Well, why not? It almost worked with Colleen, didn't it?"

"Gaelan, please," she begged, her mind barely registering what he'd just told her about Colleen and Bowen. "I don't know what you're talking about! I took Sophia to her class in Puffin's Cove, and Bowen was in the restaurant I went to for a cup of coffee. I thought it was you."

"Forget it," he said. "Don't even try." He went to the closet and pulled out his coat. Putting it on, he headed to the door. Despite her misery, Chloe noted the contrast his dark anger made against the frilliness of the room. *I will always remember him*, she thought, *silhouetted against the fog at Widow's Cliff, the wind in his hair, a faraway look in his eyes*. That thought was followed by the feeling of utter desolation. She couldn't let it happen. She let the covers drop and grabbed the robe he had only moments before so tenderly removed.

Pulling it around her, she ran to him and clutched the wool of his sleeves. "You can't go!" she pleaded. "I tried to tell you, but you said the only thing that mattered was that Sophia and I were safe." Was there a flash of doubt in those angry eyes? He looked away quickly, and Chloe grabbed at the opening, fighting for happiness itself.

"It's true I saw Bowen for the first time in the restaurant today. I thought it was you—I had no idea you had a twin brother." She spoke quickly, desperately, the words pouring out in a torrent. "He told me you didn't speak to each other, that it was because of Colleen. He said you stole her from him, but that she wasn't happy." She took a breath. "He said you might have had something to do with her death."

Gaelan took hold of her wrists and tried to pull her free, but she hung on as if her life depended on it. "It's true," she said. "He seemed so nice, and I believed him at first because of what you told me. You said you were worried that when you told me the truth, I'd want to leave right away. And I couldn't think of anything that would make me want to leave . . . So at first I thought he was telling the truth, but then I knew I couldn't believe that . . . ."

Gaelan pulled her hands free and held her wrists in a firm grip. Chloe knew she had only moments left to explain before he'd be gone and she would be left without him forever. "He said he'd like to see me again, and I said yes, because I was confused. But then the Jeep didn't start, and he offered Sophia and me a ride home. After the accident"—she swallowed hard at the memory—"he took off after the police and the ambulance came. I don't know where he is."

"Are you finished?" he said. There was no compassion or understanding in his voice, and Chloe knew he didn't believe her.

"The Jeep's in Puffin's Cove on the main street. Go see it! Then you'll see it doesn't work! Surely that would prove I'm not lying."

"I don't know what it would prove," he said coldly, "except maybe your deviousness."

Chloe felt the tears overflow her eyes and run down her cheeks. It was hopeless. He was determined not to believe her.

"Stop crying!" he said harshly. He released her wrists and, turning away from her, pulled open the door. "Do you know the worst part of your little scheme?" He didn't wait for an answer. "That the two of you almost killed Sophia in the process."

Chloe tried to protest her innocence, but the door had already slammed behind him, the echoes reverberating through the room.

GAELAN LEFT THE hotel and found the nearest pub. He didn't want to think about what had just happened, and he decided that drowning himself in Scotch would be the best method of forgetting. In the dark interior, a local Celtic rock band belted out tunes on the stage, and the audience cheered their approval. It was Friday night in St. John's, and it seemed everyone was out celebrating.

Gaelan sat at the crowded bar and ordered a double Scotch, neat. It came with ice anyway, but he didn't complain. He threw it back and ordered a second.

He was sipping the second drink when the woman next to him spoke. She introduced herself as Karen, a graduate student in anthropology at Memorial University. "Rough day?" she asked. He noted she was tall with long brown hair. Attractive, too. He started to contemplate another method of forgetting.

"You might say that," he said evasively.

"You want some company?" she said, her bright red lips suddenly close to his ear, her right breast pressed against his arm. He felt the pressure of her long leg against his thigh. He thought about it. Why not? It was becoming more and more apparent that he would never have a real relationship. Why not just series of one-night stands? Anonymous encounters to quench the desire, no strings attached.

But then the image of Chloe flashed before his eyes, the perfection of her body against the satin sheets, the taste of her mouth on his, and he knew he couldn't go through with it. That as much as he wanted to forget Chloe, he'd never do it by having sex with this woman. Or any other woman, at that. It wasn't in him.

"Sorry, I don't think I'd be very exciting tonight," he said, draining his glass. He put some bills on the bar for the bartender.

"That's okay, just looking at you is all the excitement I need," she said.

"Sorry," he repeated, getting up from his stool. "Good night."

Her own good night was lost in the cacophonous racket of the bar as he pushed his way through the crowd and toward the door. But once outside, he stood on the sidewalk, not knowing where he was going or what he was doing. He thought of trying to see Sophia, but they would never allow him in at this time of the night. He wandered the streets, the evening's events replaying in his mind until he thought he'd go insane.

By 5 a.m., he'd begun to hope that Chloe could be telling the truth. He didn't know whether it was wishful thinking, but he couldn't bear the thought that she was another Colleen, another scam by his brother. He thought back to the first time he'd seen Chloe, caught like a deer in the headlights of his car. That night, he'd assumed that if she weren't already there for his money, she soon would be. Certain she was just another gold digger, he'd compared her to Colleen from the beginning. And now, when it looked almost sure he'd been right to be suspicious, his mind was working overtime to find her innocent.

He took a taxi to the airport parking lot, where his Rolls was parked. Chloe had said to check the Jeep. He didn't know what it would prove, but he found himself doing it anyway. It took him more than an hour to drive to Puffin's Cove, only to find the street where Chloe had said he'd find the car empty. No doubt it had been towed. If it had been there at all. He drove out to the police station on the edge of town, stopping first at a Tim Horton's for a cup of coffee.

At the station, he got out of the car and read the hours posted on the locked gate. He had half an hour to wait. He leaned against the car and sipped the bitter coffee, wishing he had something for his pounding headache.

Finally, a uniformed policeman came over and unlocked the padlock on the chain that secured the gates. Gaelan crumpled the coffee cup and tossed it into a steel drum. It wasn't a big yard, only a dozen vehicles or so, and Gaelan went directly to the waiting Jeep. Windy's nephew Cullen had couriered him a spare key, which he now turned in the ignition. Nothing. She was right. It didn't work. She wasn't lying about that. But what did it prove? *The Jeep wouldn't start, and he offered Sophia and me a ride home.* It proved nothing. Bowen and Chloe could have arranged to meet in town, and when Chloe's vehicle didn't start, Bowen might have thought that with Gaelan far away, it was safe to drive her home. But for the accident, Gaelan would never have known that Bowen was even in town.

Gaelan climbed out of the Jeep and popped the hood. What he saw made him rethink his theory. Loose wires sat on top of the engine. They should have been plugged into the distributor cap, but the distributer cap was gone. This was no simple breakdown—this was deliberate!

Gaelan slammed down the hood of the car, not

knowing what to attribute the knot in his stomach to. He walked back to the station and asked the policeman where they had towed the car from the Cliff Road accident.

"It's in the yard," the cop explained. "The owner of the car took off before telling us where he wanted it towed. It's the black one with the front end shoved in."

Gaelan approached the car with trepidation. Seeing it, he realized how lucky Chloe and Sophia were to be alive. It was obvious that they'd hit the guardrail with considerable force. Gaelan also knew about the truck that had struck the rock cut. If he had anything to thank Bowen for, it was that he had managed to avoid a head-on collision with the truck.

The doors, too buckled to close, stood open. Gaelan looked into the back. A piece of paper was shoved down the back of the seat right next to the booster seat. He pulled it out. It was a drawing of a puppy, and Gaelan's eyes misted when he thought how close he'd come to losing Sophia. He folded the paper and put it in his shirt pocket before looking in the front. There was nothing unusual there, but then, he didn't really know what he was looking for.

Next he opened the glove compartment, and a shiny black object rolled out onto the floor of the car. Gaelan stood back, not quite ready to believe what he was seeing. It was the missing distributor cap. Bowen had sabotaged the Jeep and then asked Chloe if he could drive her home! Gaelan felt a surge of hope—perhaps she wasn't lying after all.

He rifled through the other things in the glove compartment and looked at the car ownership. Bowen had bought the car only the day before crashing it. With the ownership was a plastic folder—it had the name of a Greek travel company on it, and inside was the ticket receipt from Athens to St. John's via London, England, dated only two days earlier.

Gaelan looked at the little collection sitting on the passenger seat, knowing it all pointed to one thing: Chloe's innocence. So absorbed was he in his thoughts, he didn't hear the crunch of gravel behind him.

"Can I help you, brother?"

Gaelan wheeled around to see Bowen—the brother who looked so much like his own reflection but who was unlike him in every other way. Gaelan fought against the desire to launch himself at Bowen and take the smug look off his face with a good right hook to the jaw. It was probably lucky they were outside the police station—anywhere else, there was a good chance only one of them would have come out alive.

"What the hell are you doing here?" Gaelan asked.

"I came to pick up the ownership from my car. I need it to collect the insurance. A better question would be, what are *you* doing here?"

Gaelan picked up the distributor cap from the car seat and held it out for Bowen to see. "Mind telling me where you found this?"

"Ah, I see. Good detective work there, brother." His voice was full of mockery. "Don't worry. I was only having a bit of fun. I couldn't believe it. One day back in town, and I run into your new girlfriend. I thought coming to her rescue might help endear me to her a bit. She's pretty hot, you know. Have you told her about Colleen yet?"

"I notice you didn't waste any time filling her head with ideas."

"They're not just ideas, brother, and you know it— which is why you're always ready to throw a little more cash my way."

Gaelan instead threw the distributor cap at Bowen, narrowly missing him, and strode out through the gates.

CHLOE SAT NEXT to Sophia's bed. The girl was still sleeping, but Chloe noted a bit more colour in her cheeks. Unable to sleep, Chloe had been at the hospital since visiting hours started at 8 a.m. As upset as she was over the falling out with Gaelan, she could not forget Sophia. She was afraid this might be her last chance to see the little girl. She doubted she would be welcome at Widow's Cliff any longer.

She squeezed her eyes shut for a moment and willed herself not to cry. She'd done enough of that already, and her eyes were red and swollen. She had spent the better part of the night trying to make sense of what had happened. Somehow Gaelan had come to the conclusion that she and Bowen had known each other before and were conspiring together to get a hold of his money. She recalled his words: *I just can't believe I fell for the same scheme twice. First Colleen and now you. What was the plan? Marry me and then divorce me for half? Live happily ever after with my brother?*

Never had she seen someone so stubbornly hang on to his convictions. She was innocent of everything he had accused her of, and yet he refused to listen to her defence. In his eyes, she was guilty. End of story. One moment, she had come to the realization that she couldn't live without him, and the next moment, he was gone.

Oh Gaelan, she thought, her eyes closed as if in prayer. *Why did I have to fall in love with you?*

Hearing the door open, she looked up. There he was. He looked tired and drawn, and Chloe knew he hadn't slept either. Sporting a day's growth of beard, he was still wearing the same clothes. "I thought I'd find you here," he said softly. His voice was so full of tenderness that Chloe wondered for a moment if she were dreaming. He glanced over to where Sophia still slept, her breathing even and peaceful. "Can I talk to you outside?"

Chloe nodded, stood up, and walked toward him in a haze. Their eyes met, and it seemed to Chloe as if it took her forever to make those few steps. He did not step aside to let her through but instead took her silently in his arms and held her against him. Chloe let the tears flow. They came silently, soaking into the wool of his shirt.

He held her against him and took her into the empty corridor, closing the door softly behind him. "Do you think you can ever forgive me?"

Unable to speak, she nodded against his chest. He held her quietly for several minutes more, stroking her hair. When she finally raised her face to his, he gently kissed her on the lips. "I'm so sorry. When I heard you were with Bowen, I went crazy. I wanted to love you so much. Hearing that you were with Bowen was like having my worst nightmare come true. I'm sorry. I should have believed you."

"I shouldn't have listened to him," Chloe said, ashamed that she had been taken in so easily.

"Look, I know more than anyone how conniving he can be. And I didn't exactly give you any reason not to believe him. I didn't even tell you of his existence. It's I who should be ashamed of myself for not believing you. He took the distributor cap out of the Jeep, by the way."

Chloe thought for a moment. "He must have taken it when he went out to put money in the meter."

"Chloe, I know I haven't been the most sympathetic person. And I know I'm not a good father to Sophia. But if you're willing to hear me out, I'll try to explain everything. Do you think you can trust me?"

Chloe nodded.

"Then let's go home," he said before kissing her.

AS THEY LEFT the hospital, the sun was shining weakly, unusual for St. John's in April. Gaelan said it wouldn't last long. "Out here we say 'Wait five minutes,' because that's how long it takes for the weather to change." Chloe sat in the back seat of Gaelan's Rolls next to Sophia, fastening the seat belt around the child's booster seat with extra care. The events of the accident flashed through her mind, and she wondered if she would be able to relax until they were safely home.

But Gaelan drove carefully, and she soon relaxed. Two hours later, they were pulling up in front of Widow's Cliff and Windy was running down the walk as fast as her old legs could carry her.

They got out of the car, and Windy hugged Sophia as if she'd never let her go again. Chloe could see the distrust in Windy's eyes as she looked at her over Sophia, but Gaelan intervened. "It's okay, Windy. Chloe didn't do anything wrong," he said, and her suspicious look melted into one of concern for her well-being. Chloe found herself thinking of Bowen's words: *Windy is the only person in the world who thinks Gaelan can do no wrong.* It was true that Windy trusted Gaelan implicitly. Bowen wasn't lying about that.

Gaelan carried Sophia to her room, where she sat up happily in her bed, teddy bear tucked under one arm, a glass of milk and a plate of Windy's marvellous chocolate chip cookies on the bedside table. The cat was happy to see her, too, and was soon curled up on her lap, purring away. Chloe and Gaelan sat on either side of her, perched on the edges of the bed.

"Is there anything else you need?" Gaelan asked Sophia.

"Would you and Chloe stay and read me a story?" she asked. Chloe could hear the hesitation in Sophia's voice and knew the girl was not used to asking Gaelan for things. No doubt Sophia was wondering if his kindness and concern were over now that she was safely at home.

Gaelan looked down at Sophia, and Chloe could see the love in his dark eyes. But there was something else too, a disquiet that worried Chloe. Something was still bothering him. Something still stood in the way of his relationship with his daughter. Then he smiled gently, the look gone, and Chloe wondered if she had only imagined it.

"I'd love to read you a story," he said, "but I didn't get much sleep last night, and I don't think Chloe did, either." He glanced over at Chloe, who nodded her agreement. Now that they were home, there was no adrenalin left in her system to keep her going. "How about we read to you after dinner?"

"Okay," she agreed easily.

"Would you like Windy to stay with you?"

"I'm okay," she said as she reached for a cookie. Chloe watched the crumbs fall onto the quilt, knowing Windy would not normally indulge Sophia with cookies in bed.

"I'll stay for a few minutes." Windy assured Gaelan. "Then I'm going to make us all a nice dinner. Will you be eating with us tonight?"

Gaelan nodded, and Chloe knew a lot of changes were happening fast.

Outside of Chloe's room, Gaelan took her in his arms. "Oh God," he breathed against her hair. "I would love to come in and make love to you."

Beneath her exhaustion, Chloe remembered how she had felt under his touch in the hotel room before everything went wrong, and her body ached for release. He tilted her face toward his and kissed her.

"Not now," he said reluctantly, pulling himself away from her. "Later. I want it to be perfect for you, and you need some sleep. And I could sure use a shave." He smiled gently at her, and again she thought she saw the same troubled expression that had been in his eyes when he looked at Sophia. "More than that, though. I have to come clean with you. It's not a pretty story, and you have to know what you're getting into—or whether you even want to be involved with someone like me."

"Don't say that," Chloe protested and reached for him.

He placed a finger over her lips. "It's important that you hear me out. I couldn't bear for you to decide you can't stand me after all."

"I would never do that," Chloe protested.

He looked at her searchingly, and Chloe longed to reassure him. "I'll see you soon," he said. "And if you decide you still want me . . ."

Chloe nodded, knowing he wouldn't change his mind. She would have to wait. And whatever he had to tell her, she knew she could accept it.

"Okay, until later," he said, giving her a light good-bye kiss on the forehead.

In her room, Chloe stripped off her clothes with relief. She had worn them for only two days, but so much had happened that she felt like she had been wearing them forever. Grimacing with distaste, she dumped them into the clothes hamper, sure they'd never be clean again.

She rummaged through the dresser drawers and her meagre selection of clothes, remembering how Sophia had told her she should have pretty things. It was true. Except for the black silk negligee, everything was dull and practical. And she couldn't walk around in a negligee! She settled on the wool dress she'd worn on her first night at Widow's Cliff. She recalled how she had worn it with the intention of using whatever means necessary to secure her job at Widow's Cliff, with very mixed results. But it was the nicest thing she had, and she laid it over the back of the loveseat along with clean underthings and a pair of black stockings. She would go shopping for more clothes soon. It would be a nice day out for her and Sophia.

The shower was hot and soothing, and she stood under it until she thought she might fall asleep on her feet. She wrapped herself in a towel and went back across the hall to her room, crawled naked beneath the covers, and let the sound of the ocean against the rocks lull her to sleep.

As HE ATE supper with Chloe and Sophia, Gaelan remembered sitting around this kitchen table as a young boy with Bowen and their parents. There had been much laughter, much joking around, the occasional practical joke. He and Bowen had been close in their childhood, the way identical twins are, speaking their own twin language. Their differences in personality had never been an issue. When they were ready for high school, their parents sent them to different boarding schools, him to Montreal, Bowen near Toronto, and that was when they'd drifted apart. Bowen fell in with a bad crowd and opted to spend most of his holidays at school, while Gaelan had remained close to his parents and was groomed to take over the family business. And then, in his first year at Harvard, his parents had died when their private plane crashed on their way to the Caribbean for the winter. When Gaelan, the elder twin by four minutes, inherited Widow's Cliff, the bond between him and Bowen was severed forever.

Windy had made a delicious supper. The sunny day was giving way to a rainy night, but a roaring fire kept away the damp and filled the room with its comforting glow. Sophia, clearly feeling much better, ate with a good appetite. She was back to her talkative self as well, and was telling them all about the puppy she wanted, Chloe smiling at her with indulgence. Gaelan felt like he belonged to a real family for the first time since those childhood days. With Colleen, it had never felt this way.

"Do you think Cookies would like a puppy?" Chloe asked. Gaelan met her eyes across the table, and they shared a conspiratorial glance. *My beautiful, beautiful Chloe*, he thought. Could he ask her to marry him yet, or was it too soon? They had known each other for only two and a half weeks. He knew it was ridiculous.

But theirs was the typical ordeal by fire, and so long as what he had to tell her didn't scare her away . . . *No*, he thought, *we can work through this*. He savoured the thought of the three of them being a real family.

Sophia was not daunted by the prospect of her cat feeling put out. "Cookies would love to have a puppy," she said confidently. "I asked him, and he said, *miaow, miaow*. That means yes."

They all laughed together, and Gaelan hoped it would always be this way.

After dinner, Windy told Sophia it was time for bed, but Chloe protested. "We promised to read to Sophia. Gaelan and I can put her to bed and read her a story." She turned to Gaelan a little hesitantly. "Unless you have something else to do. I can read to Sophia by myself."

"Are you kidding?" he asked happily. "I wouldn't miss it for the world."

And so it was going on eight before he and Chloe were finally alone together. He stoked the fire in his office and brought out a bottle of good wine. "I thought we could talk here. It's cozier. Some of the rooms in this house are great to look at but hardly inviting to sit in."

Chloe had seen the drawing room and agreed. One felt too small in there, too dwarfed by the grand furnishings and massive paintings. She preferred Gaelan's office, with its comfortable furniture and Gaelan's nature photographs over the mantel. She sat on the couch across from the fireplace, her feet curled up beneath her.

Gaelan stood with his back to the fire, its crackling

warmth a nice contrast to the water streaming down outside the windows. One of the windows was slightly ajar, letting in a cool breeze and the smell and sound of rain. He held his glass of wine, his eyes thoughtful.

"You already know most of the story," he began. "Some of what Bowen told you is true. As the eldest son, I inherited Widow's Cliff. As far as the rest of the estate went, it was divided equally between us. It was a modest fortune by today's standards, but I put mine to work. With a bit of luck, it turned into a large fortune. Bowen, on the other hand, squandered his. He went to New York to study acting and just kept spending until it was all gone." Gaelan did not elaborate, but he suspected that cocaine was one of Bowen's many expensive tastes.

"In the meantime, he had met Colleen. She was beautiful and ambitious, and while I do believe she loved him in her own way, she was definitely not happy when the well ran dry. So Bowen had the idea to introduce her to me. It was all an elaborate scheme on their part. I didn't know until several months after we were married that they even knew each other. I know Bowen told you I kept her prisoner here, but I didn't. She was hardly ever in Newfoundland. She said she was going to auditions, but mostly she was seeing Bowen." Gaelan almost shuddered as he recalled the humiliating discovery. He took a sip of wine to give him courage.

"After I confronted Colleen, she didn't even bother pretending her interest in me was anything other than mercenary. I decided to cut my losses and throw her out. No amount of money was worth living with such a farce of a marriage. I was about to propose a divorce settlement that I felt she wouldn't be able to refuse when she announced she was pregnant." Keeping his voice flat and emotionless, he tried not to show his bitterness. He really had been happy when Colleen told him she was expecting a child. He had even hoped they might start again and have a real marriage. But it was a short-lived hope.

"So I held off on suggesting divorce," he continued. "Colleen didn't seem to be in a rush anyway. Now that she had the goose that laid the golden eggs, I don't think she really cared for the idea of a divorce. And as I said, she was ambitious. I think being the wife of billionaire businessman Gaelan Byrne was much more appealing than being the wife of penniless failed actor Bowen Byrne. And given that I was on to their scheme, she knew she would never get half my fortune like she and Bowen had originally planned on."

He took another deep breath and locked his eyes on Chloe's. "Anyway, Sophia was born, and for her sake, I tried to negotiate some sort of truce between us. But it was no good. Within a few months of Sophia's birth, Colleen went back to acting, and it was Windy and myself who were left with Sophia. I don't think Colleen had one speck of maternal instinct in her." There was a crack of thunder, and both Gaelan's and Chloe's attentions were momentarily diverted as a flash of lightning lit the windowpanes. The rain came down with a new strength of purpose, and Gaelan had to raise his voice a bit to be heard over the sound.

"When Colleen didn't show up to Sophia's second birthday party, I decided enough was enough. But the very last straw wasn't until a friend sent me a clipping from a tabloid that showed her at a party with none other than Bowen. The caption read something like, *Wife of billionaire Gaelan Byrne, Colleen, is seen here with her actor brother-in-law Bowen Byrne at a Beverly Hills party. Colleen likes to keep things "all in the family."* Anyway, that was what she was doing on her child's birthday. When she did finally make an appearance here, I told her I wanted a divorce and Sophia." He paused and took a breath. He was coming to the hardest part of the story. The part he hoped Chloe could forgive him for.

"But then she died," Chloe said gently.

"Not quite. I paid her a very handsome sum in exchange for a quick divorce and sole custody of Sophia. But before she could sign the papers, the accident happened . . ."

"Bowen thinks you had something to do with her death."

"I didn't," Gaelan said firmly. "But there is something Bowen doesn't know. Near the end, Colleen told me something. I hope it will help explain why I haven't been a very good father." He turned his back to Chloe and, resting his elbows on the mantel, buried his face in his hands. "Every time she calls me Daddy, I feel like I'm living a lie." It was so hard to just come out and say it. Except for Marcus, he hadn't told anyone, and here he was telling Chloe, the one person whose opinion of him mattered more than anyone else's. How would she feel when she learned he was keeping a secret that had such a profound effect on Sophia's life?

"What is it?" Chloe said, knowing something was terribly wrong. She got up from the couch, went over to him, and stroked his hair. "You can tell me, Gaelan. I'll understand, I promise."

He turned around and looked at her. Her eyes were full of love for him, but still, he wondered if love was going to be enough.

"Sophia is not my child. She's Bowen's."

CHAPTER 7

CHLOE STEPPED BACK, HER EYES WIDE WITH disbelief. "Sophia is Bowen's child?" she repeated. "It can't be true."

"I'm afraid it is," he said, and Chloe could hear the anguish in his voice. She longed to put her arms around him and comfort him. But first she needed to think. She thought back to her first night at Widow's Cliff.

"Is that why you don't like Sophia calling you Daddy?"

"Every time she calls me that, I feel like I'm making her tell a lie."

"Then Sophia doesn't know Bowen is her father."

He shook his head. "How can I tell her? Suppose she wanted to meet her *real* father? I can't let that happen. Bowen can never find out Sophia is his daughter!" Gaelan held Chloe's arms in a firm grip. "You do understand why, don't you?"

Chloe nodded. "I think so," she said weakly. She tried to think of what she knew about Bowen. Bowen had wasted his inheritance. He then tricked Gaelan into marrying Colleen for his money while continuing to have an affair with her. She thought back to her own encounter with Bowen. He had lied about the relationship with Colleen, accusing Gaelan of having stolen Colleen from him. He then insinuated that Gaelan had had a role in her death. He had vandalized the Jeep, played the hero by offering her and Sophia a ride home, then fled the scene of the accident. It did not add up to a very flattering picture, but did it justify keeping the truth from him? "Are you sure he doesn't have the right to know?" she asked uncertainly.

"If Bowen knew Sophia was his, he would immediately go for custody. I'm sure he'd see it as a way to get more money from me. If he got custody, I could never forgive myself. Bowen is a man who seeks out wealthy women for sex. In other words, he's a gigolo. What sort of an example is that for the child? What kinds of things would she learn, other than that sex is sold to the highest bidder?"

Gaelan was right, but Chloe didn't need much convincing. It was horrifying to think of Sophia growing up under Bowen's influence. Still . . . "But even if Bowen knew, surely no court would give him custody," she said incredulously.

Gaelan dropped her arms, but his eyes never left hers. He was pleading with her to understand. "I can't take that chance," he said. "I've gone over and over this, and every time, I come to the same conclusion. The risk is too great."

Chloe saw the result of that terrible struggle in his eyes. To think that only a short while ago she had thought Gaelan didn't care about Sophia. "You love her very much, don't you?" she asked quietly.

"As much as if she were my own daughter," he replied. "I know I don't show it very well, but it isn't because I don't love her . . ." Following closely on a rumble of thunder, lightning filled the dimly lit room with a momentary flash of brilliance. "It's just that I'm so angry about the whole mess, I think I take it out on her."

"But since the car accident . . ." Chloe began. She had seen for herself how much Gaelan had changed toward Sophia. As near as his actions came to causing a tragedy, maybe Bowen had inadvertently done something right for once.

"The car accident made me realize more than ever just how precious she is to me. It's time for me to stop dwelling on the past and move on. But it wasn't just the accident that made me come to that conclusion." He smiled at Chloe, and his eyes, which moments before had been so full of anguish, were now brimming with love. "It was you, too. I need you in my life, Chloe. Today, tomorrow, and for the rest of my life. I knew I couldn't ask you to be there for me without telling you the truth about Sophia."

Chloe nodded, her mind and heart in turmoil, trying to absorb everything he was saying to her. He was not asking her to be Sophia's teacher or even just a lover—he was asking her to stay forever. But first he was sharing with her the secret of Sophia's birth. She knew Gaelan had not trusted anyone with this before—it was far too important. But he was trusting her, and she knew it was an important demonstration of his love.

Chloe took a deep breath. She would trust him on this, just as she knew she would trust him on everything else to come. She had come to realize his true character, buried underneath all that anger: a good, honest, strong man. "I think you're doing the right thing," she said at last. "While Bowen may be Sophia's biological father, you are her true father. Because you love her and want the best for her. But . . ." And there was a *but* for Chloe. Nobody could live with a lie forever. And one day Sophia would have to be told. "I don't care about Bowen. I think you're right, he doesn't deserve to know. But one day, you will have to find some way of telling her. Sophia has a right to know who her biological father is."

Gaelan nodded. "I wish I'd always had someone in my life as wise as you, Chloe Winters," he said gently. "I'm sure my life wouldn't be the mess it is today."

He brushed back a lock of her hair that had fallen over her forehead, and she felt herself shiver under his touch. She longed for him to take her in his arms and make love to her, and she knew she would not have to wait much longer.

"Another glass of wine?" he asked.

She nodded, and he refreshed their glasses from the bottle on the mantel.

Really, in the grand scheme of things, his revelation

about Sophia was not earth-shattering. It could have been worse. It could have been something that would have made their relationship impossible—although Chloe couldn't think what that could be. She couldn't imagine anything so terrible to keep her from loving this man.

She took the glass from Gaelan, her fingers brushing his. "Here's to new beginnings," he said, touching his glass to hers. He went over to the sound system. "Something to go with the sound of the rain," he said, explaining his choice of music. "May I have this dance?"

"I don't know, I'll have to check my dance card," she said, setting down her glass once again on the mantel and slipping into his waiting arms. They fit together so beautifully. She rested her head against his chest, following the beat of his heart as much as the beat of the music as they moved slowly together. She thought back to her first night at Widow's Cliff and how she had decided she would risk everything to spend one night in his arms. It was so much better this way. To know this was not the end, but the beginning. The first night of many. The beginning of a long happy life with the man she loved. For she loved him—she knew that now.

"How is it, Chloe, that you have kept your life so simple?" he asked, his lips against her hair.

"My life has had its own complications," she said.

"Like what?"

"Like the mess with Shawn and my job."

"Yes, but if it weren't for that, I would never have met you."

"And if it weren't for Colleen, I wouldn't be here now."

"You know," he said, laughing, "it all seems worth it." He grew suddenly serious again. "But let's not talk about the past anymore. We have a future to live, and right now I just want to make love to you."

Chloe leaned against him, unsure for a moment whether her legs would be able to support her. She felt him hard against her and a moist readiness between her thighs.

He took her face in his hands, and his mouth found hers in a long, demanding kiss. She felt herself melt into him, opening her mouth to receive his searching tongue. She responded hungrily, tangling her fingers in his thick dark hair, pulling him closer against her. There was another crack of thunder, and again, lightning filled the room with its electricity, firing their kisses to new intensity.

His hands caressed her, first gently, then with rising passion as he discovered the curve of her hips. He pressed her against him with a moan. "How did I survive all these years without you?" he whispered against her mouth.

Overwhelmed with desire, she could not respond with words and instead renewed their kisses with an increased urgency. His hands found the zipper at the back of her dress, and as he lowered it sensuously, she felt his fingers leave a trail of heat down her back.

He paused, the zipper now halfway undone. "You're sure you're ready for this?" he asked seriously.

"Yes," she responded. "Don't stop now."

"Then I won't," he said huskily, kissing her deeply.

"I want to tell you something," she said breathlessly, breaking off the kiss.

He looked deep into her eyes in response.

"I love you," she whispered, with every bit of her being in those words.

"I've been longing to hear you say that." He softly kissed both her eyelids. "I love you, too." His voice was dusky and full of passion, but also gentleness. He kissed her again with renewed urgency as the rain came down even harder.

Then he lowered the fabric from her shoulders, slowly revealing the tops of her breasts. She reached behind and unhooked her bra, releasing their fullness. Her nipples were hard and ready for his touch. He stroked them with his palms. He held her against him, replacing one palm with his mouth, a moan of pleasure escaping both their lips as his tongue touched the rosy skin.

His mouth still tasting her breasts, he slipped the dress down over her hips. Her stockings and panties fell to the floor with the folds of her dress, and she was naked against him. She felt no self-consciousness; in the light of the fire, with his hands and mouth bringing her to new heights of desire, she felt beautiful and sexy. And loved.

She had never felt like this with Shawn, had never known that such pleasure was even possible. She let out a slight gasp as his hands stroked the insides of her thighs. They travelled up slowly, his fingers tracing a sensuous path, until his fingers found the soft, silky moistness of her sex. He stroked her slowly and lightly, his mouth still nuzzling her breasts, and she lost all conscious thought as the sensuousness of his touch chased everything but pleasure from her body.

Then, just as she thought she might be carried away on the waves of orgasm, he stopped and, lifting her in his arms, carried her across the office and through the door to a guest bedroom. He drew back the covers and laid her on the cool sheets. He lit the candles on the bedside table, then stood over her for a second, not touching her, but drinking in her body with his eyes. "You are so beautiful," he whispered huskily, and he began to undo the buttons on his shirt.

"Let me do that," Chloe said, not wanting to miss a moment of his touch. He leaned over her, and as she undid the buttons with trembling fingers, he traced a languid path along her body, his fingers lingering over her nipples and the soft dent of her navel before finding again the soft mound of hair and the moist warmth beneath.

As she pulled the shirt from his shoulders, his mouth travelled the same route as his fingers, and she arched toward him as he tasted her sweetness. There was another roll of thunder, and as she saw the light flash through her closed eyelids, she felt a wave of bliss that originated somewhere deep inside rolling over her, drowning her in sensation.

He encouraged her with his tongue, taking her ever higher and then releasing her, kissing her once again on the mouth, promising her that it was only the beginning. Chloe fumbled with the belt on his jeans. She unbuckled it, then found his zipper, releasing his hard sex as she slid his jeans over his hips.

A new hunger came over her as she stroked its long hardness. It was her turn to admire him, and she worshipped his naked body with her hands and mouth, revelling in the taste of his skin, the feel of his hard muscles.

He was over her now, and she parted her legs, longing to feel him inside her, so deeply that she would not know where he ended and she began. She felt his sex against her own as their mouths joined once more.

Chloe encircled his back with her arms, her hands tracing the line of his spine to the hard curve of his buttocks. "I want to feel you inside me," she whispered urgently. He loved her and she wanted to feel him deep within her, joined together.

He rose over her and he stroked the soft petals of her sex, opening them to receive him. He entered her slowly, and she felt him fill her with a satisfaction she had never felt before. They moved together slowly at first, revelling in the fit of their bodies, the sensuous feeling of the slow strokes of his sex inside her.

Then he put an arm under her and rolled onto his back so she was over him, and she felt him even deeper inside herself. He took first one nipple, then the other, in his mouth, making them hard and erect, the sensation travelling to her very core. They moved together faster and faster. Outside, the storm reached its apex — its intensity matching their own as they rose higher and higher until they came together, pleasure and release crashing over them, wave after wave.

THEY LAY CLOSE together, entwined in each other's arms, their heads close together. He planted light kisses on her eyelids and traced the curve of her still burning mouth with the tip of his finger. "That was beautiful," he whispered. "Better than I ever imagined. Where did you learn to make love like that?"

"From you," she said, kissing the tip of his finger. She had never made love like that before. Didn't even imagine such heights of pleasure were even possible.

"Hmm," he said. "You know all the right things to say." There was another rumble of thunder, this time a little more distant, and the roar of the rain lessened. "I would get our wine, but that would mean not being inside you anymore, and I don't think I could bear that."

"Neither could I. I think we'll have to stay like this forever."

"I think you're right," he said, and she felt him stir lazily inside her as he kissed her again. "Except it might make getting married a little difficult."

She broke off his kiss suddenly and looked into his eyes.

He laughed softly. "You didn't think I was just asking you to live with me?"

She hadn't really thought about it. "I don't know . . ."

she said uncertainly. All she had known was that he had asked her to be with him forever. That had been enough.

"Will you marry me?" he asked. He was not being playful now. His voice was serious. And in his eyes, Chloe could see how much he wanted her to say yes.

She felt close to tears now. Could this truly be happening to her? Surely, if she pinched herself, she would find it had all been a dream. She would wake up alone on her cousin's couch in Boston, the sound of the rain and the ocean in reality nothing but the sound of the street-cleaning machine that had invaded her sleep so often in the past.

"I know we haven't known each other very long," he said reassuringly. "If you like, we can have the wedding in the fall. Although I would prefer May."

"May," Chloe whispered.

"Then that's a yes?" he persisted.

"Yes," she managed before the tears spilled over.

Kissing her tears, he held her close. "Thank you," he said.

They lay there for a while until Chloe's tears subsided. "Sorry," she said finally. "I thought it was only in romance novels that people cry when they're happy."

"Don't apologize. It's beautiful. Are you sure one month is enough time to get ready for a wedding?"

"I don't know. I've never been married before." She tried to think of the women she'd worked with who had married. They had spent at least a year planning their day. Bridal showers, dresses, seating arrangements, invitations, music, flowers. By the time the actual day arrived, they had been exhausted with all the planning. Chloe knew that wasn't the kind of wedding she wanted. She wanted something simple, but special. Something she would enjoy and remember.

She explained this as best she could to Gaelan, and he agreed. "Just family and a few close friends. Although I do have some business associates who would probably be offended if I didn't invite them. I'd like Marcus to be the best man."

Chloe responded to the suggestion with silence, not because she objected to Gaelan's choice but because she couldn't help but think of Bowen. He, she knew, would not be invited. Suddenly it struck her as sad that he should be so estranged from his only brother—a twin, at that.

"You don't mind if Marcus is the best man, do you?" he asked.

"No, of course not. I was just thinking of Bowen."

Gaelan's eyes grew hard at the thought of his brother. "He was the best man at my wedding to Colleen, you know. I did it partly out of obligation, as we had grown distant by that point—who doesn't have their twin as their best man? But now he's the last person I want at my wedding."

"I know," Chloe said sympathetically. "I just think it's sad you have to be such enemies. He is your brother."

Gaelan sighed, his eyes softening. "I know. I wish it

could be different. We were best friends when we were children, even though we're so different." He raised his head and propped himself up on his elbow. "It was when our parents died and Bowen learned I was the sole heir to Widow's Cliff that all the trouble started. He didn't think the minutes separating our births were enough to establish me as heir. He felt Widow's Cliff should be sold and the proceeds equally divided. I promised to compensate him for his share, which I have, many times over. But he was determined that if he couldn't own Widow's Cliff, neither could I. I refused to sell. This house is part of my family's heritage—it's more important to me than all the money combined. I can't begin to know how Bowen thinks, but it seems to me he's been determined to get revenge ever since. I don't want to be enemies with my only brother, but I don't think it will ever change. His hatred is not about Widow's Cliff anymore. It's irrational and obsessive." There was a faraway look in his eyes, and Chloe knew that if there were any way he could make peace with his brother, he would.

"It's too bad," Chloe whispered.

Gaelan let his head drop back. "It is," he said, "but I really don't want to talk about Bowen right now. I want to talk about our wedding and how we're going to live happily ever after."

"Okay," she agreed. "Where were we?"

"We were talking about asking Marcus to be the best man. Aren't you supposed to have a best girl or something?"

Chloe laughed and kissed him quickly. "Maid of honour, silly." She thought carefully for a moment. "Does Marcus have a girlfriend?" she asked.

"Kathryn," he said. "You'd like her."

"Let's ask her. As Marcus is your closest friend, I have a feeling we'll be seeing a lot of them."

"Good idea. Kathryn is great. I'm sure you'll soon be good friends. But don't you have a friend or relative back in Massachusetts whom you'd like to ask?"

She thought back to Boston. "All my friends sided with Shawn in the breakup. I was pretty lonely by the time I left. And I don't have any close female relatives other than a few aunts I don't know very well, and they all had boys. So Kathryn would be perfect. And Sophia, of course, will be the flower girl."

Gaelan smiled at her suggestion. "Do you want to hire someone to plan the wedding for us?" he asked. "It would make it easier."

"Okay," Chloe said, feeling immediately relieved. "But it has to be simple, and I'd like to have it here at Widow's Cliff. I mean, if that's what you want." She didn't want to sound like a pushy bride-to-be. It was his day, too.

"Whatever you like, just so long as you're the bride and I'm the groom."

"That's the only thing I really need," she said.

"We could elope," he suggested playfully.

"My parents would never forgive me," Chloe said. She wondered how they were going to react to her getting married so soon. Chloe tried to put herself in their position, knowing they would be shocked Chloe was marrying a man she hardly knew. But she also knew that in the end, her parents would support her decision and be happy for her. And they were going to love Sophia. Chloe knew they would accept Sophia as her own grandchild and probably spoil her terribly. She smiled at the thought.

"A penny for your thoughts," Gaelan said, tracing the shape of her smile with the tip of a finger.

"I was just thinking of my parents and how much they're going to love Sophia."

"How do you think they'd feel about more grand-children?"

"Our children?" Chloe asked. Everything was moving so fast. She was still processing the idea of being a wife, let alone a mother.

"Of course *our* children, darling." He took his finger from her lips and kissed her instead. "And after what we just did, who knows? It could happen in about nine months."

Chloe blushed, realizing that safe sex and birth control had never even entered her mind. It wasn't like her to be so irresponsible.

"Don't worry, I'm completely safe, and unless you don't want children . . ."

"No, of course not. I'd love to have your children," she said with utter sincerity. Then she laughed. "How many would you like, Mr. Byrne? Six, ten, twelve? You know how much I love children, and there are certainly enough rooms in this place."

"How about we start with one?" he said.

"That's okay, too," she said. She touched her flat stomach and wondered if, at that very moment, a child was beginning to form in her womb. She hoped so. She pictured them as a family in a year or so. Lying on the bed, baby or babies—didn't twins run in families?—at her breast, Gaelan beside her, Sophia playing happily with her cat. She felt so utterly happy and blessed. Never in her wildest fantasies did she imagine her life could have taken such a fairy-tale turn. Schoolteacher from the city meets billionaire in the castle. Not that it mattered to her that Gaelan was rich. She would marry him no matter what he did. Farmer, shopkeeper, shoe salesman . . . The last one made her smile again. Gaelan as a shoe salesman was pretty absurd. It was like imagining Mr. Rochester in Charlotte Brontë's *Jane Eyre* selling shoes.

"Another smile. What for this time?"

Chloe didn't think she could explain what that smile was about. "Just happy," she said.

"Me too," he said as he began to trace a finger along the curve of her cheek, exploring the hollow of her throat. "I was wondering if you'd like to go back to teaching after we're married. I'm sure you'll want to be more than just Mrs. Gaelan Byrne." She looked at him, and he hurried on. "You don't have to teach. You can do whatever you like."

"It's not that," she said. "I was just wondering how I would teach Sophia, too."

"Maybe it's time to send Sophia to a school with other children," he said thoughtfully.

Chloe approved. "I think that would make Sophia very happy. You never know, maybe I could get a job at the same school." She smiled at him mischievously. "That is, when the twins are old enough."

He laughed. *This, Gaelan Byrne,* he thought as he kissed her deeply, *is all you could ever want.*

CHAPTER 8

MAY BROUGHT SUNSHINE. MORE, GAELAN said, than Newfoundlanders were used to—spring usually took its own sweet time coming to the Rock. Off the headland, icebergs shone in the sunlight, dazzling mountains of icy blue jutting out of the open water. Gulls dove at the water's surface in search of food, and the air was fresh and salty. The ice pans that had clogged the water only a few weeks before were now a memory, and a boat could be seen chugging through the white-tipped waves.

"Horses dancing on the bay," Gaelan said, seemingly out of the blue.

"Pardon?" Chloe said, scanning the water and wondering what he could possibly be referring to.

"Horses dancing on the bay. It's a Newfoundland expression for whitecaps. Windy uses it all the time."

"I like it," Chloe said as she watched the waves roll in. "Why don't you have a Newfoundland accent like Windy? Even Sophia has a bit of one."

"Boarding school," he admitted. "Bowen and I spent

most of the year at school. I was in Montreal, and Bowen went to Toronto. Then I went to university in Boston, and he headed to New York to act. I was only home for the holidays and summers, Bowen even less."

"I can't believe we might have been in Boston at the same time! Though I did grow up on Cape Cod. Did you like it? Being away at school so much?"

He looked at her, and Chloe could see a flash of sadness in his eyes. "It was pretty lonely—I wouldn't send any child of mine away to school," he said with conviction.

Despite the sun, it was still far from warm, and Chloe turned up the collar of her coat against the wind.

"Getting cold?" Gaelan asked, his voice full of concern. He took off one of his gloves and felt her cheek before unwrapping the cashmere scarf from his neck and placing it around her own. "Is this better?" he asked, taking her into his arms.

"Perfect," she answered as she settled into the warm circle of his arms. Her back to him, she rested her head against his chest. "This has to be the most beautiful view in the world."

"I'm so glad you agree," Gaelan said. "Some people find it too wild for their liking . . ." His voice trailed off, and Chloe knew he was thinking of Colleen. She reassured him that she was as much in love with Widow's Cliff as he was.

"Did you know," he said, "that Leif Erikson discovered Newfoundland five hundred years before Columbus ever set foot in America? He called it Vineland the Good, and there were Viking settlements here for centuries.

There's one near here—it's quite a tourist attraction. If you'd like, I'll take you there someday."

"I would like that," she said. She had bought a history of Newfoundland in Puffin's Cove on the day she'd met Bowen. It was fascinating, and she was anxious to see more of the province and the places she had read about with their quaint names like Blow Me Down, Twillingate, and Placentia Bay.

Beside them on the ground was an empty wire cage. Earlier that morning, they'd gone to the vet in Puffin's Cove and picked up the bald eagle that she and Sophia had rescued on the cliff. The vet had said the bird was finally well enough to be released, and Sophia had insisted on being the one to set it free. Chloe felt it was an important moment, not just for Sophia, but for them all. A shared experience that united them as a family. Gaelan had brought out his camera to record the event and promised to hang one of the photos in his office.

On the trip from the vet, the bird had sat patiently in its cage and regarded them without fear. Sophia said it was because the bird remembered them and knew they had saved him. She spoke to the bird, advising him in a reassuring and confidential tone to stay away from bad men with guns.

They opened the cage on the headland between the house and the cliff. The bird did not fly away immediately. Instead, it perched on the edge of the cage unhurriedly, taking in its new surroundings. It looked healthy and strong, its feathers sleek and shiny, the proud black eyes peering clear and alert out of its hood of white feathers. It was hard to imagine this bird had once been on the brink of death. Careful not to make any sudden moves, Gaelan took several pictures. The bird stood so still, Chloe could have sworn it was posing for the camera. Then at last, it spread all five feet of its great wings—hesitantly at first, as if testing them—before finally lifting off and flying toward the ocean.

Sophia waved and called goodbye over and over as the bird circled higher and higher above them. And the bird seemed to say goodbye too, its shrill cry carrying on the wind.

When the bird was only a black speck against the sky, Gaelan continued to snap pictures, but now it was Sophia he was trying to capture on film. Framed by her wind-tossed blond curls, her expression was one of poignancy. Chloe guessed that while she was delighted to see the eagle healthy again, she felt at the same time a sense of loss as the bird flew away from them. Chloe felt it too and said a silent prayer for the bird's safety.

Sophia was soon looking for another distraction and, inspired by the wind, went into the house and came back with materials to make a kite. She tied a string to the handles of a plastic grocery bag, and as she ran along, the bag filled with air and billowed out behind her. She was obviously delighted with her creation, and Chloe marvelled at how a child with all the toys she could ever want could also be happy with something so simple.

Chloe sighed. If there was any blight on her happiness,

it was the secret of Sophia's parentage. She felt so much sadness for Gaelan and understood his struggle to accept the truth. How terrible it must have been to learn the daughter he loved so much was really the product of his wife's infidelity. And with his brother, at that!

"What was that sigh for?" Gaelan asked, planting a kiss on top of her head.

"I was just thinking how much simpler it would be if Sophia weren't Bowen's."

"I've been thinking that for years. Unfortunately, it doesn't change the facts."

"I know," Chloe said resignedly, turning around in the circle of his arms and looking into his dark eyes. "I've been thinking we should talk to a child psychologist. I'm sure you're not the only father in the world who has this problem."

He touched the tip of her nose with his finger before planting a light kiss on it. "There you go again."

"What do you mean?"

"Being so wise. I knew I put myself in good hands."

She laughed off his compliment, but was flattered all the same. She liked that he respected her opinion where Sophia was concerned. And she was pleased she had made such a difference in how he related to Sophia. His love for the child was so much more evident now, his affections, while still a bit awkward, so much more easily given—a far cry from the days when he couldn't bear to be called Daddy. Chloe couldn't help but be proud to have played a role in this process.

A shout rang from the house, and they turned to see Windy calling them for lunch. They, in turn, called to Sophia, and she came running over, colliding into Gaelan as she came to a halt. She was breathless, her cheeks flushed and rosy. Gaelan released Chloe and caught Sophia up in his arms, lifting her, laughing, into the air.

Gaelan set her down, and with an arm around Chloe and a hand holding Sophia's, they walked back to the house together where Windy served up some of her famous clam chowder.

It had been three weeks since Gaelan had asked Chloe to marry him, and the wedding was Sophia's favourite topic of conversation. She'd already picked her flower-girl dress with the help of Renée, the wedding planner Gaelan had hired in Paris. She'd also chosen the flowers she was to carry, and Chloe was surprised by the girl's good taste. The wedding had become the favourite subject of Sophia's drawings as well. She drew pictures of Chloe in an array of different fairy princess dresses.

"I've been wondering," Sophia said, stirring her soup thoughtfully. "Now that you and Daddy are getting married, am I supposed to call you Mommy?"

"If you like," Chloe said, exchanging a smile with Gaelan. They were lucky. Sophia had accepted Chloe as her new mother without hesitation.

Sophia rested her elbows on the table and, supporting her face in her hands, scrutinized Chloe across the table. Her face contorted into comical shapes as she mulled over the problem.

"I will call you Chloe until you and Daddy get married. Then I'll call you Mommy," she concluded. She sipped her soup from her spoon, her busy mind at work over a new problem. "It's a good thing the wedding is not at a church," she said a few moments later.

"Why's that?" Chloe asked.

"'Cause if it was at a church, Cookies wouldn't be able to come. I don't think they let cats into churches."

"We hadn't thought of that," said Gaelan with a wink at Chloe. "But it is a good point."

Sophia chewed thoughtfully on a muffin, and Chloe somehow knew she had an agenda in mind. "If I had a puppy, he could come to the wedding, too."

Gaelan and Chloe laughed together. So much for the wedding being the favourite topic of conversation. Sophia was not going to give up on the puppy, and Chloe knew she and Gaelan were going to have to discuss it. Sooner or later they were going to have to tell Sophia yes or no. Chloe liked the idea of making this decision with Gaelan, as she liked everything about her new role as mother.

Sophia continued. "You put the wedding rings on the pillow, and the puppy carries the pillow in his mouth. I saw it in a movie."

"What happens if the puppy chews the pillow and swallows the rings?" Gaelan asked.

Sophia dropped her spoon into her soup and shook her head at Gaelan in exasperation. "You have to train the puppy, you silly," she said with exasperation.

"Your Daddy—silly?" Windy exclaimed with mock indignation as she passed a slice of buttered bread to Sophia. "You're the one who's as foolish as old socks. Imagine a cat and a dog at a wedding! As if my nerves weren't skinny enough as it were!"

"You're an old sock," Sophia said to Windy as she stuffed the bread into her mouth.

"I think you're a pair of old socks," Gaelan said, regarding both of them with indulgence.

Sophia laughed at Gaelan's joke. "You're an old sock too," she hooted. "And Chloe. We're all old socks."

Gaelan got up from the table, shaking his head at Sophia. He had to attend a meeting in Puffin's Cove and was already running late. He had proposed a joint venture between Byrne Enterprises and the town to address the current unemployment problem. Fishing had once been a way of life on the island, but the stocks of cod were now depleted, and a generation of young people whose families had for centuries fished off Newfoundland's Grand Banks were continuing to face an uncertain future. Gaelan, whose love of the island extended to its people, was passionate about bringing them a more prosperous future.

Gaelan gave Sophia a goodbye hug. "Do you need anything while I'm in town, Windy?"

"No, thanks. My nephew Cullen is picking up groceries for me later."

"Chloe?"

"No, thanks," she said, getting up. She was on her

way to the ballroom to see if Renée, the wedding planner, needed any help. "But I'll walk you to the door," she added.

"You didn't ask me if I needed anything," Sophia called after them.

"I'm sorry, honey," he said. "What would you like?"

"A puppy!" she announced triumphantly.

Chloe walked with Gaelan across the hall to the front door. "You know, we're eventually going to have to make a decision about that puppy," Chloe said.

"I know," he said. "How about we make it a wedding present from us to Sophia? That way she'll have something to amuse her while we're away on our honeymoon."

"Sounds like a great idea," Chloe said. They were going to Paris for their honeymoon. It was only for a week, but Chloe felt bad about leaving Sophia behind with Windy.

They kissed goodbye, and Chloe watched Gaelan drive out of sight. She was glad he was only going to Puffin's Cove. He would be back by supper, and she looked forward to spending a quiet evening with him. Last week he had gone to Montreal for two days, and to Chloe it had seemed a century.

It was something she knew she would have to get used to. While she could sometimes accompany him on business, she knew it wouldn't always be possible, especially when she had Sophia to care for. She would have to get used to spending at least some time away from him.

She touched her lips where he had kissed her and felt a shiver of expectation for the evening ahead when they would end up in his bed—their bed—and find new ways to delight each other until they fell asleep in each other's arms.

She murmured another prayer of thanks for all the happiness that had befallen her. Gaelan as her husband, Sophia as her child, Widow's Cliff as her home. And there was one other thing. She touched her flat stomach with her hand and prayed also that it was true. Her usually regular period was now four days late. She would know for sure by the wedding day. It would be her wedding present to Gaelan. The best one she could possibly imagine.

IT RAINED FOR almost two weeks. Rain and wind and fog so thick they could be cut with a knife. And while the day of the wedding dawned clear, the forecast was for snow. Snow—on the last day of May.

Chloe took a long hot bath, wrapped herself in a bathrobe, and sat at her dressing table drying her hair. Not in the master bedroom suite she now shared with Gaelan, but in her old room, the one she had stayed in when she first arrived at Widow's Cliff. She glanced at the full-length mirror and remembered how she had stood in front of it in her long black negligee, thinking she would sacrifice everything to have one night in Gaelan's arms. Back then, it had never crossed her mind that she would stand at the same mirror in her wedding dress. Not one night, but *until death do us part*. And she was not sacrificing anything but rather gaining everything. Gaelan, a home, a daughter, and, she thought, placing her hand over her stomach, *this new life*, conceived on the first night they'd made love. She had found out for sure yesterday. She had gone to the clinic in Puffin's Cove, and her heart had leapt with joy when the doctor congratulated her on the test findings. It had been so hard not to call Gaelan right then and there, but she was determined to keep this as a surprise for the night of their wedding.

Downstairs, caterers were busy preparing food in the kitchen, flowers were being delivered, and last-minute decorating was taking place while Renée went around giving orders with military precision. But despite all this activity, it was strangely quiet. Windy and Sophia had gone to Windy's sister's house, where they were getting ready. They could have prepared just as easily at Widow's Cliff, but Sophia was so excited that she was constantly in the way.

Gaelan had flown to his San Francisco office a couple of days before to deal with another emergency. She had been disappointed he had to leave so soon before the wedding. *Just think*, he had said, *the next time you see me I'll be waiting for you to come down the aisle*. It was a lovely image, and she comforted herself with it as she lay in the big empty bed at night. His trip had one practical element. He promised to arrive in his private jet at the same time as her parents' flight was due in from

Boston via Halifax, and drive them in his Rolls. Chloe glanced at the clock on the dressing table. They would be more than halfway to Puffin's Cove by now. Renée had booked a bed and breakfast for Gaelan and Chloe's family, and they would dress there before heading out to Widow's Cliff.

The three hours before the wedding stretched ahead of her like an eternity. She didn't need any longer than twenty minutes to get dressed. Twenty minutes to do her makeup, and another ten for her hair, which she had insisted on doing herself. Renée had told her to be ready at one thirty sharp, when Marcus's girlfriend, Kathryn, Chloe's maid of honour and only bridesmaid, would join her before they came downstairs together. She still had two hours to kill.

Her dress was hanging on the front of the wardrobe. Unlike the elaborate fairy-tale creations in Sophia's pictures, it was simple and elegant, in creamy silk. She knew she looked wonderful in it, and she couldn't wait for Gaelan's reaction.

Chloe heard a knock on the door and called out for whoever it was to come in. She had expected Renée, but the woman standing in the doorway in a long fur coat and tall black boots was a complete stranger. About thirty-five, tall, and rail thin, while she looked to be naturally blond, her hair was bleached almost white from the same sun that had left her looking too tanned for a Newfoundland spring. Marcus's girlfriend? She had not yet met her bridesmaid and had no idea what she looked like, but she hadn't imagined her looking like this. "Kathryn?" she asked hesitantly. She approached the woman, ready to hold out her hand and introduce herself, but the woman shook her head.

"No, I'm not Kathryn," she said a little impatiently. "Who's Kathryn?" Chloe felt the woman look her up and down, and she held the dressing gown tightly around her.

"My maid of honour. I've never met her before. So I thought—"

"Isn't that that a little unusual? Having a woman you've never met before as your bridesmaid?" The woman closed the door behind her, and Chloe caught the heavy scent of expensive perfume.

"She's the best man's girlfriend," Chloe explained. She wanted to say it was none of this woman's business, but she didn't want to offend one of Gaelan's business associates. At least, she assumed this woman was one of his business associates. She couldn't imagine him having a friend this rude.

"I see," the woman said without any particular interest, her icy blue eyes now taking in the room around her.

Chloe didn't know why, but the woman immediately unsettled her. Perhaps it was because wealth hung around her like an aura, and Chloe felt suddenly like the poor country cousin. Strange, really, that she should feel this way when she was about to marry one of the wealthiest men in North America. But then, it wasn't his wealth she had fallen in love with, and she still hadn't quite grasped the idea of being rich. Sometimes she wished Gaelan didn't have any money—at least then he wouldn't have to go away so often on business.

"I almost thought that French woman wasn't going to let me see you. She's pretty possessive of this whole affair," the stranger said with a sudden hint of humour. She looked much more human when she smiled.

Chloe attempted a smile in return. "Renée's our wedding planner. She just wants everything to be perfect."

"Well, the dress sure is perfect," she said, examining the wedding gown with an experienced eye.

Chloe nodded, feeling irrationally pleased that this unknown woman approved. She held out her hand to the woman and introduced herself. At least she had someone to talk to for a while. It would make the time go faster.

The woman took her hand briefly. Her hands were manicured to perfection, and she wore a large opal on her ring finger. "Cassandra Belcaro." Chloe didn't remember the name from the guest list, but there were so many unfamiliar names on it that she was hardly surprised.

"How do you know Gaelan?" Chloe asked.

"Oh, Gaelan and I go a long way back," she said with a dismissive wave. "I must say, I was surprised to hear he was marrying again. How long have you two known each other?"

Chloe blushed slightly, recalling her mother's reaction on the phone to their very brief acquaintance. "About two months," she said.

"Rather quick, don't you think? Are you sure you know him well enough?"

Any feeling of friendship toward the woman quickly evaporated.

"Gaelan and I have the rest of our lives to get to know each other," she said a little haughtily.

The woman arched her well-shaped eyebrows. "Spoken like a true woman in love," she said with a sigh and a sad nod of her head. "Or maybe lust."

Suddenly Chloe felt very angry. What gave this woman the right to cross-examine her like this, business associate of Gaelan's or not? Chloe was very close to asking her to leave.

Cassandra continued. "I was hoping to speak to Gaelan before the wedding, but I was informed by that French woman he is en route from the airport with your parents."

"Yes. He was returning from a business trip to San Francisco at the same time and kindly offered to drive them."

Cassandra nodded dismissively. She walked to the loveseat in front of the fireplace, where a small fire burned on the hearth, and sat down. She unbuttoned her coat, revealing a short black dress. Then, taking out a compact from her bag, she checked her flawless makeup.

"It doesn't matter," she said, putting her compact away. She looked at Chloe and shook her head slowly at her. "It's probably better I talk to you anyway."

Chloe felt suddenly uneasy. She had felt nauseous

that morning, but put it down to the excitement of the wedding, or even a touch of morning sickness. Now she felt it again. She knew that whatever this woman was about to say to her wasn't going to be good. She wished she had the nerve to tell her to leave.

"I'm assuming that since you don't know your own maid of honour, you don't know a whole lot about Gaelan?"

"I know enough," Chloe said staunchly.

"Has he ever mentioned he was married before?"

"Yes."

"What did he tell you about her?"

Suddenly Chloe didn't care if she offended one of Gaelan's friends or business acquaintances. This woman had no right to interrogate her, and she was sure Gaelan would not tolerate this if he were here. "I don't know that it's any of your business," she said firmly.

"Maybe not," Cassandra said with a slight shrug, "But I do think you have a right to know the truth."

"I do know the truth," she said confidently.

"You mean Gaelan's version of the truth."

"Of course," she said. "Who else's? Bowen's?"

Cassandra looked surprised. "So you know Bowen? I can't imagine Gaelan telling you Bowen's side of the story."

"I've met him," Chloe said warily.

"And did he tell you about himself and Colleen?"

Chloe didn't answer. She felt trapped in her own room. The clock on the dressing table ticked away the seconds as it counted down to her wedding. She was approaching what was to be the happiest moment of her life. So why did she feel this impending sense of doom? She glanced at the door and wondered if maybe she should just walk out herself.

Cassandra clearly took Chloe's discomfort for a yes. "I suppose Gaelan disputed everything Bowen told you."

"Of course," she said. She remembered the day she had met Bowen and how she had at first thought he was a nicer version of Gaelan. He had told her about Colleen and how Gaelan had stolen her away from him. She recalled how he insinuated that Gaelan had played a role in Colleen's death.

"Did it ever occur to you there might have been a grain of truth in Bowen's version?"

"No," Chloe said sharply.

"I think the lady doth protest too much."

"Look," said Chloe, genuinely angry now. "Did Bowen send you here? Because if he did, I want you to leave right now. I don't want to hear any more of his lies."

Cassandra laughed. "Bowen didn't send me here. I haven't seen Bowen in years. And to tell you the truth, I'm not sure what Bowen made of Colleen's death. Although I'm sure he didn't agree with the official verdict that it was an accident."

Chloe went over to the window and looked out over the ocean, unseeing. It was clear Cassandra had come to tell her something about Gaelan, and she had the impression she was not doing it out of kindness. She would hear her out only because she didn't know how to make her leave, and when Gaelan arrived, she would tell him what had happened. She couldn't believe that he would invite this woman to their wedding.

Still standing at the window, Chloe spoke. "Why don't you just tell me why you're here? Because in case you hadn't noticed, I'm getting married, and I have to get ready." No matter what this woman said, Chloe was not going to let her ruin the wedding. She turned to face her.

"Okay, okay." Cassandra lounged back against the arm of the loveseat, a fur-clad arm draped along the back of the seat. She crossed her long, elegant legs and patted the seat beside her. "Why don't you come over here and sit by the fire?"

Chloe shook her head. "No, thanks," she said coldly. "I'm fine here." The last place she wanted to be was sitting next to this horrible woman.

"I don't suppose you'll believe me if I tell you that this is for your own good. I think you have a right to know what kind of man you're marrying."

"I do know," Chloe said angrily.

Cassandra gave her that patronizing look again. "I know, I know. Now hear me out. Gaelan told you Colleen died when she fell from the cliff. Is that right?"

"It was an accident. There was an investigation into her death."

"You know there are other theories. Her body was never recovered—you do know that, right?"

"I hope you're not going to sit here and tell me that

Gaelan played a part in her death. Because if you are, you can get out. I've heard it all before from Bowen."

"Does Bowen think Gaelan pushed her off the cliff?" Cassandra sounded genuinely taken aback for a moment. "I suppose I shouldn't be surprised. Bowen always liked to think the worst of Gaelan. Still, I am surprised he didn't suggest suicide. That was another theory going around."

"It doesn't matter what Bowen or anyone else thinks," Chloe insisted. Bowen had definitely suggested suicide as a possibility. "It was an accident."

"How would you react if I told you it was none of those things? Murder, suicide, or accident?"

The room seemed suddenly quiet. There were no other possibilities, were there? Murder, suicide, accident. What else could there be?

Cassandra uncrossed her legs, stood up, and went over to the fire. She held out her hands toward the flames for a moment. "I'd forgotten how cold this bloody island can be in May," she said as she turned toward the window. "Look out there. It's the first of June tomorrow, and it's snowing."

Chloe glanced out the window, barely registering the large white flakes. "What happened, then?"

"There was no accident," Cassandra said at last, her brightly painted lips curving into a smile.

Chloe stood still. She had no idea how to begin to process what she was hearing. "What do you mean?"

"Just what I said. Colleen didn't fall from the cliff."

"Then how did she die?"

Cassandra looked at Chloe, and for a moment Chloe thought she could see pity in the woman's eyes.

"Are you sure you don't want to sit down?" she said, almost gently. "This might come as a bit of a shock."

"For the love of God, just tell me, then leave me alone!"

"Perhaps a bit of background will help you understand better. You do know that Colleen and Bowen were lovers before she married Gaelan."

Cassandra's story was the same as Bowen's. Colleen and Bowen were lovers until Gaelan had stolen her away from him. He was possessive and overbearing. She was unhappy.

She paused. "Is this sounding familiar? Is this what Bowen told you?"

Chloe nodded wearily. "Yes, I've heard this all before."

"Bowen doesn't know the rest of this story. Colleen never had the chance to tell it to him. Colleen told Gaelan she wanted a divorce. He was furious and refused. He couldn't bear the thought of Colleen going back to Bowen. And so he made her a deal." Here Cassandra straightened up and stared directly at Chloe, who couldn't tear her eyes away.

Cassandra continued. "He would let her go, but on the condition that she disappear, become a new person, and never see Bowen again. He promised her a large sum of money to go away. And she took it. It seemed like a way out. She was heartbroken about leaving the child, but she knew Gaelan would never let her get custody." Cassandra was stony-faced as she talked, her face betraying no emotions. "She decided it was time to wipe the slate clean—pretend she had never met either of the Byrne twins, never lived at Widow's Cliff, never had a child." Cassandra sighed. "So she went to Italy, changed her name, and started a new life for herself."

She stared at Chloe long and hard as she stood up. "Do you understand what I'm saying to you?"

Chloe looked at her blankly, the feeling of nausea coming back. She could hear the sound of her own breathing and prayed this was all a nightmare. Soon she would wake up, and it would be her wedding day. A wedding day like this one could only exist in a terrible dream.

"Who are you?" said Chloe, her voice sounding strange and faraway to her own ears. She didn't need to ask, though. She already knew the answer.

The woman pulled herself up to her full height. "I'm Colleen Byrne, Gaelan Byrne's wife."

CHAPTER 9

HIS FRIENDS WOULD BE AMUSED. GAELAN smiled in the mirror at the sight of himself in a tuxedo. Rarely had his friends ever seen him in anything other than jeans, and this was as formal as they come. A jacket with tails. He looked like he was ready to step into a movie set in Victorian England, the kind with a tall, dark, broody hero who mopes around the moors. Not that he looked broody today. How could he, when in just a few hours, he and Chloe would be husband and wife?

He was in his suite at the bed and breakfast in Puffin's Cove that Renée had booked for Chloe's family. Her mother and father were in the next room getting ready, and elsewhere in the house were a handful of her aunts, uncles, and cousins.

He had enjoyed getting to know Chloe's parents, Adèle and Doug, in the car. They were gentle people whose lives had been primarily occupied with their jobs and their child. It was going to be great having them as his in-laws, and it was nice to be part of a family again.

Adèle and Doug had held hands in the car, and Gaelan was touched by their devotion to each other after almost forty years of marriage. He liked to picture himself and Chloe forty years from now holding hands, still as much in love as they were now.

He couldn't wait to see Chloe again. Despite the fact that he had spoken with her several times, these two days away from her had been torture. And as much as he was looking forward to the ceremony and the chance to publicly state his vows to her, he couldn't wait for the day to be over and for them to be alone. They would leave Widow's Cliff after the reception and stay in St. John's before flying on his jet to Paris the next day.

The night before, he'd had a long talk with Marcus, who'd agreed to take on even more responsibilities in the running of Byrne Enterprises, freeing up Gaelan to spend his energies on his more philanthropic endeavours, the things that made a real difference in the world, the things he loved to do. But most importantly, it would give him more time with Chloe and Sophia. Until now, he had filled his days with work and sought to fill the void in his life by building Byrne Enterprises. But all that had changed since Chloe had arrived. It was time to let someone else do the work. He had a life now.

Thanks to Chloe, he knew now he loved Sophia like she was his own child, and he always would. Still, he would like more children—his and Chloe's. Sons and daughters to carry on Byrne Enterprises and Widow's Cliff. He would have to be wiser than his father in dividing up his estate—he didn't want his children to fight over property the way he and Bowen had. He sighed. He didn't want to think of Bowen now. This was his wedding day. A new beginning.

Gaelan put on his long black cashmere coat over the tuxedo, the image in the mirror suddenly more familiar. He ran his fingers through his unruly waves and went to collect Chloe's parents for the ride out to Widow's Cliff.

Already it was starting to snow, big wet flakes like a Christmas card. The owners of the B&B congratulated Gaelan as he left the house, cautioning him to drive safely. "Only in Newfoundland," they said with stoic shakes of their heads. "A May wedding in the snow."

The roads weren't too bad yet, and the trip to Widow's Cliff went smoothly. It wasn't until they arrived that things started to go wrong. Gaelan knew something was amiss the moment he saw Marcus waiting anxiously inside the front door. Gaelan introduced Chloe's parents to him and, after leaving them in the capable hands of an usher, allowed Marcus to steer him to his own office, where they would wait until Renée told them it was time to go to the ballroom.

"*Mon dieu*, Gaelan! I've been trying to reach you, but your cell was off."

Gaelan pulled his cell out of the pocket of his long coat. "Damn, I must have forgotten to turn it on after I got off the plane. What was it you needed me for?"

"It's Chloe," he said.

Gaelan felt a sudden panic as he imagined a dozen

different scenarios, none of them good. "Oh God, she's okay, isn't she? She's not sick, is she?"

Marcus put his hand on Gaelan's shoulder. "Calm down. There's no need to panic." Marcus went to the mantel and poured a small measure of Scotch. "Here, drink this. Chloe, like you, is probably just suffering from nerves."

Gaelan swallowed the drink obediently, thinking that until Marcus had decided to scare him to death, he had been as cool as a cucumber over the whole thing. "So, what do you mean by nerves?"

"Well, Kathryn went up there just over an hour ago to meet her, but Chloe refused to let her in. She told Kathryn she wanted to speak to you before the ceremony. Renée and I went up and tried to talk to her through the door, but she wouldn't even answer us."

Gaelan nodded and handed Marcus his empty glass. "On second thought," he said, reaching for the glass again. "Pour me another one. Maybe this is all Chloe needs." Gaelan took the drink. It didn't seem like Chloe to behave this way, but then, maybe it was to be expected. She was about to marry a man she had only known for two months, not to mention one with a six-year-old child. Maybe panic was the most sensible reaction a woman could have in this situation. "How much time do I have?"

Marcus looked at his watch. "Twenty minutes. Renée wants you ready to go in half an hour."

"Okay, I'll be back."

Gaelan took the stairs at the end of the hall two at a time and knocked on Chloe's door. "It's me, Chloe." There was no answer, and again he felt that pang of fear. Perhaps Marcus was wrong. Maybe it was more serious than a case of nerves. He tried the door. It was unlocked, and he opened it slowly to let himself in, closing it softly behind him.

He looked around the room, taking in the wedding dress still hanging on the wardrobe. Renée had said it was bad luck for the groom to see the dress before the wedding. He had laughed but gone along with tradition. Until now.

He didn't see her at first. But then he noticed a pair of stockinged feet protruding over the arm of the couch facing the fireplace. She must have fallen asleep. After all, she should be dressed by now, ready to go downstairs. He approached the couch slowly, not wanting to startle her when she sat up.

Gaelan froze. He couldn't believe his eyes. This must be a nightmare.

"How sweet," she said. It was a voice he never thought he'd hear again. "I could use a drink about now."

Gaelan dropped the glass. It bounced on the carpet, and Scotch splattered the hem of his pants. "What the hell are you doing here?"

"It's nice you still recognize me after all these years." She leaned over and picked up the glass at Gaelan's feet. "Shame about the drink, though. First time I've ever seen you waste good Scotch."

"You're supposed to be—" He stopped. Really, he wasn't totally surprised. This was why he had hired those private detectives.

"I know, I know. I also know it caused quite a stir. Did the billionaire kill his wife? Drive her to suicide? Or was it an accident after all?"

"Why the hell did you do it?"

"What?" she said innocently, getting up from the couch.

"Stage your own death. That's what you did, isn't it?"

"Something like that—I am an actress, after all. Besides, I couldn't let Bowen get his hands on the money. You know what they say about a fool and his money being soon parted. And I always thought leaving before the divorce was final might come in handy one day."

She was standing very close to him, and yet Gaelan felt as if the whole thing weren't real. It wasn't that he wished Colleen was dead, but he certainly hadn't cared ever to see her again. Especially on the day he was marrying the woman he loved.

"Where's Chloe?" he demanded, not wanting to spend another moment with this woman. "No wonder she wants to speak to me. I take it you've introduced yourself, and she's now wondering what the hell is going on."

Colleen lifted one of her shoulders in an elegant shrug. "I don't think Chloe wants to speak to you."

"She told Kathryn she wanted to speak to me, and that's what I'm going to do. I don't know what little game you're playing by being here today, but I have every intention of marrying Chloe in the next hour."

"I don't know if that's possible. Can you marry Chloe when you're still married to me?"

Gaelan felt himself nearly blinded with anger. He had never struck anyone in his life, let alone a woman, but he felt dangerously close to it now. "You—" he started to say, but he couldn't finish. What could one possibly call someone this conniving and evil? "Don't even think of interfering in my wedding," he finished in a low voice.

"You know that part in the wedding when the minister asks if anyone objects? I figure that's my cue." She smiled coldly.

Gaelan had no idea what to do now about the ceremony. If he went forward with it, was he committing bigamy? Plus, he had no idea how to stop Colleen from carrying out her threat. And if he was upset, he couldn't imagine what Chloe must be going through right now. God knows what Colleen told her. He grabbed Colleen by the arms, shuddering at the touch of fur and the thin arms underneath. "Where is she, Colleen?"

"I don't know, darling. She didn't tell me where she was going. She did put on her coat, though."

Gaelan let go of her arms abruptly, and they dropped limply to her sides. He turned and strode for the door. He opened it, looking over his shoulder at this woman he hadn't seen in four years. A woman he had once been married to. The mother of Sophia. She had made his life a misery once before, and he'd be damned if he'd let her do it again. "You stay here—I'm not done with you yet!"

He slammed the door behind him and ran back downstairs to his office.

"Thank heavens you're back!" Renée said, leaping up from the couch. Renée, Marcus, and Kathryn gathered around Gaelan.

"Is everything okay?" Kathryn asked anxiously.

Gaelan shut the door behind him, leaning against it for a moment as if to regain his strength. "*Okay* is hardly the word I'd use," he said.

They listened in stunned silence as he quickly filled them in. When he finished, no one spoke.

"I should have told Chloe I suspected Colleen might still be alive," Gaelan said finally. "I was going to, but, well, I think I convinced myself I was only being paranoid. And I just wanted to put it behind me."

Marcus was the first to recover. "Yes, and I think I had something to do with that decision. But God knows you paid enough private detectives to try to locate her."

Gaelan straightened up. "You're right." This was definitely a time for action and not for wallowing in past mistakes. The most critical thing was to find Chloe as soon as possible. He turned to Renée. "This is going to take major damage control. You're really going to earn your fee on this one, Renée. First, I want you to find Chloe's parents. Tell them that Chloe has gone for a walk, and I've gone to look for her. Let them stay here in the office and assure them I'm doing everything I can to find her." Gaelan strode back and forth in front of the fireplace, his brow furrowed as he took control of the situation. "Then I want you to find Windy. She's pretty level-headed. Get her to stay with Chloe's parents."

He turned to Kathryn. "Can you please help Renée on this?"

Kathryn nodded earnestly.

"Sophia is with Windy," Gaelan continued. "She'll need to be told something. Keep it simple. Then get Windy to call her nephew. He has a puppy for Sophia at his house. Have him bring it over now. That should keep her distracted."

He stopped pacing for a moment. "Renée, you're going to have to make some sort of announcement to the guests."

"What do you want me to tell them?" Renée said desperately. "This is a little out of my league."

"Tell them there's a delay because of the weather. We're waiting for someone—they don't need to know it's the bride. Get the orchestra to play. Get the caterers to bring out food and set up the bar. That should keep everyone happy until I know one way or another whether I'm getting married today."

He turned to Marcus, knowing he was really indebted to his partner and friend for this one. "Marcus, get my lawyers on the phone. Ask them if I can go ahead with the wedding, then deal with Colleen. I imagine you'll find her in Chloe's room. She didn't show up just to ruin my wedding—she showed up because she thinks she can get more money out of me. A second divorce settlement or something."

"Maybe I'm stupid, but I don't understand this," Kathryn interrupted. "You gave Colleen the money for the divorce settlement before the divorce was final?"

"No, it was I who was stupid. The money was in trust with my lawyer. He gave her the money before she finalized the divorce. I discovered she was sleeping with my lawyer, too." Gaelan sighed and shook his head. "Needless to say, he isn't my lawyer anymore."

"So you're still married to her?" Kathryn asked.

"Exactly."

"Oh no," she said quietly.

"Just imagine how Chloe must feel right now," Gaelan said. He did up the buttons on his coat. "I've got to find her. He opened the door, and they could hear the guests in the hall laughing and talking, oblivious to the fact that the bride had run away. "One last thing," Gaelan said to the room in general. "Say a prayer that she'll forgive me."

CRYING, CHLOE WALKED down the bluff, following the fence that guarded the edge of the cliff. Around her, the snow swirled, but she barely noticed. She couldn't even remember how she came to be out here, conscious only of wanting to put distance between herself and Widow's Cliff.

She did remember getting dressed. Under Colleen's scornful gaze, she had thrown on her jeans and a sweater, barely taking the time to grab her coat—the beautiful green coat Gaelan had given her—before fleeing down the back stairs of the house and slipping out the side door. She needed to get away from Colleen, from the house full of guests, and to make sense out the terrible mess that had become her life. First the whole fiasco in Boston with Shawn, when she lost her job. And now this. Her fairy-tale ending was turning into the ultimate horror story.

She tried to focus on the facts. Everything Colleen had said contradicted Gaelan's version of events. But it matched what Bowen had told her. According to Bowen and Colleen, Gaelan had stolen Colleen from Bowen. According to Gaelan, Colleen and Bowen had plotted together to get his money.

She had believed Gaelan at the time, accepting that everything Bowen had told her was a lie. But now? What was she supposed to believe now that Gaelan had lied about Colleen's death? All along he had made love to her knowing that Colleen was alive. Here she was marrying a man who already had a wife he was hiding in Italy!

She stumbled over a rock hidden in the snow, falling to her knees. In the distant reaches of her brain, she acknowledged the pain and stood up again. She wiped the snow absent-mindedly from her jeans with her bare red hands, then put them back in her pockets.

She kept walking, her head bent into the snow and wind. No. It didn't make any sense. There was something she didn't know, some piece of the puzzle that was missing. What did Gaelan gain from hiding his wife from her? Not only did it not make sense, it just didn't fit with the Gaelan she had come to know these past months.

Gaelan was not a man who was comfortable with secrets. She had seen how he had struggled with the secret of Sophia's parentage. How it had torn him apart to withhold from Sophia the truth. She had seen him come to peace with it too, and seen how he was able to show his love for Sophia now as much as if she were his own.

Chloe also knew how much he had tried to resist her, afraid that she was like Colleen, after his money, not his love. He could have had her as his lover that very first night, but he didn't.

A gust of wind whipped the snow into a frenzy, and she raised an arm to protect herself from the stinging precipitation as she tried to make sense of everything.

More than anything else, Chloe was sure of one thing. Gaelan loved her. She felt his love to the very centre of her being. The way he looked at her, the way he treated her, the way he made love to her, the way he wanted to share the rest of his life with her. And then there was this baby, conceived in love. She knew how happy he would be when he found out.

If he loved her enough to entrust her with the secret of Sophia's parentage, he would also have trusted her with the secret of his wife. If Gaelan had known Colleen was alive, he would have told her. She remembered what she had said to him when he found out she had been fired from her job. She told him he shouldn't be so suspicious.

Now it was time she took her own advice. She would trust the man she loved. Really, the only thing that made sense was that Gaelan would be as shocked as she was when he learned Colleen was still alive. She would go back. He would explain everything, and then she would marry him.

She wiped away her tears. Her decision made, she finally looked around her for the first time since leaving the house. It was hard to see. The wind drove the snow into her face, blinding her as she tried to penetrate the wall of white swirling around her. For the first time, she noticed that she was cold, very cold. But that was okay, she was going home now—soon she would be back in front of her fireplace, where it was warm. She would put on her dress, and she and Gaelan would be married.

She turned around and reached out for the fence that would guide her back, but her hand found only air. She edged over, sure that the fence could only be steps away, but still there was only the snow-filled emptiness. How long had she been wandering around out here? She looked down and realized she was standing in her own snowed-in footsteps. Circles! She was going in circles!

BACK AT THE house, Gaelan checked the garage for the Jeep first and was relieved to see it still there. He didn't like the idea of Chloe driving in the storm. But then he didn't like the idea of her being on foot either. He looked at his watch. She had been gone for an hour, and the temperature was dropping. He hoped she had had the presence of mind to put on a warm coat.

Head bent into the wind, he walked around the house and across the headland to the fence. He looked over the edge of the cliff but could not see the ocean below, only a bottomless pit of churning snow. He was glad the fence was there—in this weather, it would be only too easy to step over the edge into nothingness. He shuddered at the thought.

The storm was getting worse. Up until now he had been mainly concerned about her mental state, but now he was more worried about her physical safety. He knew only too well how dangerous storms could be. They were disorienting, and it was absolutely true that people could walk around in circles for hours. But hypothermia was the real problem. Once the body temperature started to drop, sleep became only too tempting. To sleep was to die. He had heard of people freezing to death only yards from their front doors.

His heart clenched with fear. He needed more help.

He pulled his cell out of his pocket and called the police station in Puffin's Cove. He asked for the chief, David Carpenter, a man he had known since childhood. During the investigation into Colleen's "death," David had been steadfast in his conviction that Gaelan was innocent of any wrongdoing. Gaelan didn't explain to him that Colleen was back from the dead, only that his fiancée was upset and had gone out into the storm. "I'm getting worried. I'm searching the grounds of Widow's

Cliff right now, but I'm wondering if she might have taken the road in the hopes of getting a ride. Can you radio the snowplows to be on the lookout for her?"

"Sure, Gaelan. I'll send out a patrol car to check the road between Puffin's Cove and Widow's Cliff, too."

Gaelan thanked him and put his cell back into his pocket. He looked behind him. Already his footsteps were filled with snow. There was no hope that Chloe's tracks would still be visible. He walked along the fence, calling her name every couple of minutes. They had often taken walks along here, and Gaelan hoped she had chosen this direction again.

CHLOE LOOKED DOWN again at her tracks in the snow. She was lost. She panicked and spun around, seeing nothing but swirling snow in every direction. Which direction was home? And how far was it? A mile? Two miles? She listened for the sound of the ocean. If she kept the ocean on her left, she would find her way home, she reasoned. But all she could hear was the wind and her own frightened breathing. She was lost!

She started to run, stumbling forward in the snow, running until she was out of breath, only to see her own snowed-in footprints. Three sets of footprints — all her own! Blankly, she looked down at her green coat. It was covered with snow, and she had the terrible feeling she was disappearing into the landscape. Her and the baby. She staggered on, shivering uncontrollably now. Out of fear. Out of cold. Going on blindly in any direction—to keep moving was her only goal. How long had she been walking?

The longer she walked, the more unreal everything became. Just like a snowstorm in May, everything that had happened today seemed impossible. It was like a dream. A horrific dream. Colleen. This snowstorm. This cold. *Yes, that's it*, she thought, becoming slowly calmer. *A dream*. She would wake up soon, Gaelan would be there, and she would put on her wedding dress, and they would get married.

She saw him like a mirage or a vision, herself and the swirling snow reflected in his dark eyes. She walked toward him. She wouldn't wait for the wedding; she would tell him about the baby now. She didn't want to forget. It was, after all, her wedding present to him.

She opened her mouth to speak to him, but suddenly the vision was gone. She looked around for him, but there was only snow. Suddenly, she stumbled against a boulder. She reached out, and her hands touched the sharp branches of a tree. She realized she had wandered into a small copse.

For a moment, she thought she heard her name being called. She stopped and listened, but it was only the wind playing tricks on her. "Gaelan?" she said. She tried to shout, but the name was all but lost on the wind.

She crouched down between some boulders. It wasn't as windy here. And she wasn't cold anymore. She was just sleepy. She would just close her eyes, and when she woke up, she would be next to Gaelan in their bed, and she would tell him about their baby . . .

GAELAN HAD BEEN walking for almost an hour when his cell rang. He reached for it, praying it was Marcus saying Chloe had returned to the house unharmed.

"Gaelan, David here."

"Yes," Gaelan said anxiously.

"Sorry, Gaelan. No news, I'm afraid." The connection crackled, and Gaelan lost the sound of the chief's voice for a moment. "Are you still there, Gaelan? I can't do much before this storm lets up. But if she's not back by then, we'll see if we can't get a search party organized."

"I hope that won't be necessary," Gaelan said, fearing if he didn't find her before then, it might be too late. Already there were more than six inches on the ground, and the storm showed no indication of letting up before nightfall. Chloe had already been out here for two hours. In this cold and wind, hypothermia was a real possibility. He put the phone back in his pocket and continued to follow the fence away from the ocean, calling her name in between praying for her safety.

Suddenly, he remembered that near here was a small copse of trees surrounded by large rocks. On this wind-swept headland, it was the only place that could be considered shelter. The snow was blinding, and as he could see no farther than a couple of feet, he relied on his sense of direction and intuition to guide him. Again he called her name, and again heard only the wind in reply. He pressed on in the direction of the copse, head bent into the wind and snow, knowing he could pass within feet of the trees and never see them.

More and more he feared she was hurt. Surely, if she were out here, she would be returning his calls. And if she wasn't here, where was she? He prayed she had not gone beyond the fence. Outside the grounds of Widow's Cliff, the edge was not protected by a fence, and in this weather, it would be only too easy to step off . . . He shuddered and tried to block the horrifying image from his mind. But there was a terrible irony to the scenario— to find out his first wife did not die from a fall from the cliff, only to have Chloe . . . He could not even finish the thought.

What would he do if he lost her? He could not imagine his life without her. Only a couple of months ago, he had been determined never to fall in love with another woman. Now, here he was, more in love than he had ever thought possible, his life changed forever. Never could he have imagined such happiness with another woman. No god could be so cruel as to snatch her away from him. He saw his life stretched out before him, an eternity of missing her, an eternity of wishing for her.

He stopped suddenly, sure he heard the faintest of sounds on the swirling snow. He raised his head and listened again. Only the wind. But instinct told him to follow the sound, and he turned to find that he had been about to overshoot the copse by just six feet.

He walked between the trees and boulders, his heart nearly stopping when he glimpsed the dark green fabric of her coat beneath a dusting of snow. *Oh God*, he breathed, *let her be alive*! She was curled up in the fetal position, one arm tucked under her head. Her eyes were closed, the snow white against her lashes.

Gaelan didn't breathe. He pulled off his glove and touched her cheek. She stirred, and her eyes opened.

"Gaelan," she whispered.

Gaelan felt relief flood over him. She was alive! She was probably suffering from minor hypothermia, but she would be okay. "You're safe now," he said, his voice catching, tears of relief filling his eyes.

He took off his coat and wrapped it around her. He knew he was risking exposure himself, out in this wind and snow in only his wedding suit, but he knew Chloe needed the extra warmth. They were possibly two miles from the house, a distance too great for him to carry her. Both of them needed warmth quickly.

He took out his cell once again. "Marcus. I found her. I'm close to the road here, where the fence meets the road. Get out the Jeep and meet us. Fast."

STRIPPED OF HER frozen clothes and wrapped in blankets, with a roaring fire blazing in the fireplace, Chloe lay on the bed in the master bedroom suite. Gaelan's doctor, a guest at the wedding, had already been in to see her. She had asked to speak to him alone, and he reassured her there was no reason to fear for the safety of the baby. And it was with tears of relief as much as pain that she cried as the circulation returned to her frozen feet and hands. Chloe felt she could bear almost anything so long as the baby was safe. Gaelan held her in his arms, giving her sips of warm tea, stroking her hair, talking to her gently until the tears subsided and the shaking stopped.

She took a long hot shower, and after a meal of toast and tea, she felt almost normal again, at least physically.

"I've ruined our wedding," she said apologetically to him at last.

"No," he said. "It was me who was at fault. I should have told you I suspected that Colleen really didn't die in that fall. You see, my lawyer had given her a great deal of money. But after her so-called death, there was absolutely no trace of it. I was suspicious and hired private investigators to search for her. I only recently decided I was being paranoid and called off the detectives. I didn't tell you about it because I didn't think it was an issue anymore." Gaelan stopped and looked thoughtful for a moment. "That lawyer must have helped her hide the money and change her identity."

"No. It's my fault," Chloe insisted. "I should have just trusted you. If I had done that, I would have just told you she was here and trusted that you knew as little about it as I did." The tears welled up in her eyes once more. "Gaelan, I love you so much. I'll never mistrust you again. No matter what anyone says."

He held her to him, unable to answer, his eyes full of tears of gratitude and love. How did he ever come to deserve this woman's love?

There was a light knock on the bedroom door. "It's me, Marcus. May I come in?" Not quite in charge of his voice yet, Gaelan murmured his permission. He had been so concerned with Chloe's safety, he had almost forgotten that Marcus had been left to deal not only with Colleen but also with a houseful of storm-marooned guests and Chloe's anxious parents.

"Really, Marcus. After this, I'm going to have to give you a raise."

Marcus smiled at him. "Your gratitude is all the thanks I need," he said jokingly. Like Gaelan, Marcus was dressed in tails, and he gave a mock bow, flicking the tails behind him in a comic gesture. They all laughed, glad to find some comic relief in the situation.

Marcus picked up one of chairs in front of the fire and turned it around to face the bed. "I think," he said as he sat down, suddenly serious again, "all things considered, you're going to be pretty happy after I give you the lowdown on my chat with Colleen."

"Good," Gaelan said with relief.

Before embarking on a description of his discussion with Colleen, Marcus smiled gently at Chloe. "I'm happy to see you're feeling better."

"I'm sorry I worried everyone," she said meekly.

"Don't apologize. That was a terrible shock you had. We're all just glad you're safe." An hour after the wedding was to begin, Marcus had felt it was time to tell the guests that Chloe was missing. The mood had turned immediately sombre, and Marcus had the terrible thought that the wedding might turn into a funeral. Marcus had never considered himself to be a religious person, but he prayed then to anyone who might care to listen.

"But I feel bad," Chloe said. "All these people came to the wedding, and now they're stuck here."

"I wouldn't worry about them," he said. "Now that they know you're safe, they're having a great time. Your mother and Windy are already best of friends, and Sophia is so happy with her puppy, I don't even think she's noticed that things haven't gone according to plan."

"I really do appreciate everything you've done today," Gaelan said, thanking Marcus again before asking him what happened with Colleen.

"Not much, really. By the time I spoke to her, I think she realized that she had really gone too far this time. So I told her we could ruin her in a legal battle or she could simply agree to sign the divorce papers. Your lawyer faxed them over, and she signed them without protest. They now await your signature."

"She didn't mention more money?" Gaelan asked, surprised. Everything with Colleen had always come down to money.

Marcus shook his head. "You know, I don't even

think she was here for more money. From what I can gather, she's done quite well with the money you gave her. Perhaps this isn't exactly the time to say this, but I felt a bit sorry for her by the time she left. She's a pretty unhappy woman. I think she got a short-term high out of shocking you and Chloe, but in the end she seemed to realize it was a pretty empty victory. I think she sensed how much you both were in love and how very much alone that made her."

Gaelan was silent for a moment. "You could be right," he said. "She's a bitter woman. In the end, she even cut off Bowen." But Gaelan had an even greater concern. He tried to tell himself it wasn't that it was easier when he thought Sophia's mother was dead, but this was going to be difficult to explain to the girl. "Did she want to see Sophia?"

Again Marcus shook his head. "No. I'm not even sure the child exists to her."

It was hard to comprehend a woman having so little feeling for her own child, and Chloe vowed to herself that she would make up for it by being the best mother she could to Sophia. "Where's Colleen now?" she asked.

"She asked if I knew where Bowen was. When I told her he was still in Puffin's Cove, she asked me how she could get to him. I told her it wasn't safe to drive, but she insisted on going. In the end, Windy's nephew took her in his four-wheel drive. I bet Bowen was pretty surprised to see her."

"I bet he was. And you know, despite all their faults,

I think they really did love each other, until their greed got the better of them. Who knows, maybe after all these years, those two have learned their lesson."

Marcus shook his head in amazement. "That is incredibly charitable of you after all they've put you through. I'm more inclined to say that misery loves company."

"I don't know," Chloe said. "I hope they can be happy together. He is your brother, and she is Sophia's mother."

Gaelan sat down again on the edge of the bed. "You're the one who's wonderful. After everything you've gone through . . ." He kissed her hair.

"But what are you going to tell Sophia?" Marcus asked.

"We'll tell her in time," Gaelan said, looking at Chloe. "We'll find a way." With this wise, beautiful woman at his side, everything would be okay.

Suddenly the door opened, and Sophia herself burst into the room, a wide-eyed spaniel puppy pressed to the breast of her silk flower-girl's dress. *Poor Renée*, Chloe thought. *She must be on the verge of a nervous breakdown by now.* This had to be the craziest wedding ever.

"Daddy!" Sophia cried. "Thank you for the puppy!" Gaelan swept her, puppy and all, into his arms. "Daddy," she protested. "You're squashing us!" Gaelan laughed and set her down again on the floor, listening attentively as she praised every aspect of the dog. One day Sophia would have to learn the truth about her parents, but not today.

When finally she stopped, she noticed Chloe wrapped in her dressing gown on the bed. "Why aren't you dressed?" she asked in a puzzled voice. "You and Daddy have to get married. Everybody's waiting."

Gaelan searched quickly for an explanation Sophia could understand when Chloe said, "You know, I feel so much better now. It would be a shame not to get married today."

"Are you sure?" Gaelan asked, and Chloe could hear the excitement in his voice.

"More than ever," she said quietly. "It may not be exactly the wedding we planned, but I don't think I could stand another minute of not being your wife."

Gaelan turned to Sophia, smiling "Looks like your puppy is going to get to come to the wedding after all."

CHLOE KNEW SHE would never forget a moment of her wedding. The guests had cheered as she and Kathryn walked down the aisle. A beaming Sophia following behind, puppy clasped in her arms, flowers long forgotten. She and Gaelan exchanged vows and walked back up the aisle amid thunderous applause. She threw her bouquet to Kathryn. She had caught it, and Marcus had rewarded his girlfriend with a kiss. Chloe hoped they would be as happy together as she and Gaelan were.

It was well past midnight by the time they reached the honeymoon suite of their hotel room in St. John's. The storm had let up by early evening, allowing the plows to clear the roads. They had driven to St. John's through a winter wonderland, a shimmering blanket of white under the stars, so strangely marvellous at this time of year.

Gaelan picked her up and carried her over the threshold, dropping her onto the bed and falling down beside her. "Mrs. Byrne, I don't think I have ever been so exhausted in my whole life."

Chloe drew herself up on one elbow and looked down into his eyes. "That's a pity," she said slyly. "Because I still had some wonderful plans for the evening."

He reached up and started to unbutton her coat, drawing it off her shoulders, his finger tracing a tantalizing trail down her back. "I will never be too exhausted for this," he said, kissing her, a long, deep kiss that Chloe returned with all the love and passion she felt. When he broke away, his eyes were full of a deep tenderness, his voice both gentle and serious. "When I saw you out there in the snow, and I thought I'd lost you . . . I didn't think I could go on living. I love you so much, Chloe. I know it may sound a little clichéd, but I do mean this with all my heart. You have made me the happiest man in the world today."

"Only the world?" she said softly. "Because I think I can do even better than that." She leaned over and whispered her wonderful news into his ear. "We're having a baby, my love."

Epilogue

I T WAS A GLORIOUS DAY FOR A FIRST WEDDING anniversary, and a perfect day for a picnic. The breeze was warm, and fluffy white clouds sailed across a brilliant blue sky. What a contrast to their wedding day! Across the green grass of the headland, violets bloomed, their fragrant scent combining with the saltiness of the ocean.

Supporting herself on one elbow, Chloe lay on her side on the quilt next to Ryan and Rory, who reached up with their little hands as if they could catch the clouds. They laughed and gurgled and tried again while Chloe watched them with amazement. What had she ever done to deserve such happiness? They were four months old now, and Chloe still couldn't believe that these two gorgeous little creatures were hers. Twin boys, hers and Gaelan's. They were identical, with Gaelan's dark hair and eyes. Gaelan joked that while they looked like him, it was lucky for them all that they had inherited their mother's good nature. And they were dreams. Happy and contented, the only thing that could upset them was being apart.

A few feet away, Gaelan gazed over the ocean, lost in thought. The light danced off the waves like diamonds spilled by the sun. Below, the white surf rolled off the rocks, the sound sweeter than any music. He was thinking about Bowen. He had shown up at Widow's Cliff only two nights before, and when he'd left, Gaelan had known it would be a while before he processed everything that had happened.

When he had answered the front door, he had been shocked to see Bowen. He had not spoken to his brother since the day in the police yard when he discovered that Bowen had tampered with Chloe's Jeep. He had pretty much written him off after that. He eventually heard that Bowen was living in New York with Colleen, just like the old days, before they'd hatched their plot to get their hands on Gaelan's money. A part of him had hoped they were happy together. Bowen was his twin, and looking at his own babies and the bond between them, he knew he could never be fully free of his brother.

Gaelan had let him in the foyer, closing the door behind him. "What do you want, Bowen?" he asked. He assumed Bowen had come to ask for money, as he had so many times in the past.

Bowen leaned against the front door, looking down at his feet. "I know you don't want me here, but I didn't know where else to go." His voice was quietly desperate, and Gaelan heard the intake of his breath like a sob. He knew then that this wasn't a simple request for money. Something, he knew, must be terribly wrong, and he felt an instinctive desire to comfort his twin.

"What's wrong, Bowen?" he asked gently.

It took several minutes before Bowen could compose himself enough to talk. "Colleen's gone, Gaelan," he said as his voice cracked again. "And this time, she won't be coming back."

Gaelan stiffened at the sound of Colleen's name. "She left you?" he asked without much surprise. Colleen had always been on the lookout for greener pastures, and Gaelan figured that going back to the perpetually broke Bowen had not been her first choice.

But Bowen shook his head. "She died last week, Gaelan." His voice was barely a whisper.

Shocked, Gaelan didn't know how to react. "Are you sure?" he said. After all, Colleen had supposedly died before.

"She died in my arms, Gaelan. It was cancer. She had just been diagnosed when she heard you were getting married. I think that's why she came back . . ." His voice had trailed off.

Now Gaelan looked down the cliff to where the water pounded against the rocks, rolling back into the ocean in its tireless battle to wear away the island. He recalled the look in his twin's eyes. The look of anguish, grief, pain, regret. "I'm sorry," he said to Bowen.

"I know you don't believe this—but I loved her,

Gaelan," Bowen managed to say, and Gaelan took his brother into his arms and comforted him.

They had talked late into the evening, and Gaelan had the sense they were on the road to being brothers again. Trust would come later, but it was a start. He realized now how much he had missed Bowen. He thought of Rory and Ryan and how they couldn't bear to be apart. He and Bowen had been like that once.

As for Colleen's death, he was surprised at his own sadness. Not just for her death, but also for her life. He didn't wish that level of bitterness on anyone. He sighed and watched as a gull dove into a wave and emerged with a shimmering fish. One day he would have to explain all this to Sophia. He prayed he would find the way to tell her about this woman who'd been her mother in name only.

But Bowen had brought good news too. He remembered the puzzled look on Bowen's face as he spoke. "There was something Colleen wanted me to tell you."

Gaelan braced himself.

"She said to tell you that you're really Sophia's father. Did she tell you that you weren't?"

Gaelan remembered how he had nodded calmly, a hundred different emotions threatening to overwhelm him.

"She never told me that," Bowen said. "Didn't you have paternity tests done?"

Clearly, it had not crossed Bowen's mind that Colleen had named him as the father. And paternity tests meant nothing when the potential fathers were identical twins.

Bowen had eventually left, and Gaelan went to his and Chloe's room. Chloe had been awake, feeding Rory and Ryan. It was when he told her that the news really sank in. He was Sophia's father! Her real father!

Gaelan looked down the headland to where Sophia was playing with her puppy. Not really a puppy anymore, Snowstorm had grown to his full size. He could hear her laughter floating on the breeze and said a small prayer of thanks that this wonderful child was really his. One day he would have to explain the strange, sad story of her mother, but at least he didn't have to tell her he wasn't her father. For that, he could be thankful.

He watched the sun dance on the waves and felt suddenly at peace. There was so much to be grateful for, so much to be happy for. His home, his children, and his wife. Especially his wife. He turned to where Chloe lay next to the twins on the blanket. She looked up at him and smiled, and he felt a lump in his throat. God, how he loved her!

He watched as Chloe got up from the blanket and walked toward him, the breeze lifting her long, white, gauzy skirt. He held out his arms to her, and she slipped into them, her body fitting into his, so familiar now, but at the same time so exciting. He thought ahead to the evening. After the children were in bed, they would share a bottle of wine to celebrate their anniversary and afterwards they would make love. He thought of the years ahead of them, and he knew they would always be like this, their love deepening with the passage of time.

Chloe looked up at him, and he could see the love in her eyes. "You've been far away," she said softly.

"I'm back now," he said, holding her even tighter in his arms.

There was a shout, and they turned to see Sophia running toward them, Snowstorm at her heels. "Mommy, Daddy!" she called as she neared. Gaelan released Chloe and swept her up in his arms. It felt so good to hear her call him Daddy and know that she was truly his. And as for calling Chloe Mommy—well, Chloe was everything a child could want in a mother.

"What is it, honey?" he asked.

"Look out on the water!" He turned around, and together they all focused on the ocean. "Dolphins!" Sophia exclaimed, pointing to a school of dolphins jumping gracefully through the waves, water glistening on their backs. "Get Rory and Ryan," Sophia said, struggling out of Gaelan's arms.

Gaelan set her down and went over to the blanket, returning with a baby in each arm. He planted a kiss on each of their dark heads. "Do you see the dolphins?" he asked them for Sophia's benefit. The babies reached out toward the water with their little hands and made their lovely baby sounds.

"See the dolphins, babies," Sophia said in the special quiet voice she reserved for her little brothers. "We'll tell Grandma and Grandpa about them later." Chloe's parents had moved to a little house in Puffin's Cove to be nearer to their grandchildren, and Doug was now helping Gaelan run his charitable foundation while Adèle frequently babysat.

Chloe stood at Gaelan's side, tucking her arm through one of Gaelan's, her fingers brushing Ryan's soft hair. Gaelan turned and kissed her tenderly. They watched as the dolphins frolicked in the waves. "Happy?" he asked her softly.

Chloe nodded, her heart too full to speak, while overhead the call of an eagle came like an answer on the wind.

About the Author

Meadow Taylor is the author of *Midnight in Venice*, *Christmas in Bruges*, *Falling for Rain* and *The Billionaire's Secrets*, and is the pen name for a pair of Ontario-based authors of historical fiction. Visit Meadow online at https://www.facebook.com /meadowtaylorbooks.